# FEARLESS

# Fairy Tales

By Konnie Huq & James Kay

Illustrated by Rikin Parekh

Piccadilly
PRESS

# IMPORTANT NOTE

Due to the risk of paper cuts,
please do not use pages of this book to wipe your bottom
when you run out of toilet paper.

# CONTENTS

$$e^{i\alpha} = \cos\alpha + i\sin x \qquad G_{\mu\nu} = 8\pi G(T_{\mu\nu} + \rho_\wedge g_{\mu\nu})$$

$$e^{i\pi} = \cos\pi + i\sin\pi$$

$$\int_a^b f'(x)dx = f(b) - f(a)$$

$$e^{i\pi} = (-1) + (0)$$

$$\boxed{e^{i\pi} + 1 = 0} \qquad 1 = 0.99999999999999999999999$$

$$a^2 + b^2 = C^2$$

$$\frac{d}{dt}\left(\frac{\partial L}{\partial \dot{q}}\right) = \frac{\partial L}{\partial q}.$$

$$A(u) = \int_\Omega (1 + |\nabla u|^2)^{1/2} \, dx1 \ldots \ldots dx_n.$$

$$t' = t \frac{1}{\sqrt{1 - \frac{v^2}{c^2}}}$$

$$V - E + F = 2$$

$$A = \frac{1}{2}bh$$

$$P = 4a$$

$$b \times h \quad l \times h$$

$$P = 2(l + b)$$

$$E = mc^2$$

# SLEEPING BRAINY

Oona was a very brainy princess. She could count to seventeen million and do her forty-eight times table backwards. (She could do it forward too, mind you, but she found that a little too easy.) She knew Einstein's theory of relativity[1] inside out and was even working on a new and improved version. To say Oona was *quite* clever was an understatement – like saying Rapunzel's hair was *quite* long. The truth is, Oona was a flipping genius!

---

[1]   A very important maths thing to do with space and time and, well, everything.

Oona already knew exactly what she wanted to be when she grew up, and it most certainly was *not* a princess. She couldn't imagine who in their right mind would want to spend their days tiara shopping or leafing through *Vanity Fairy Tale* magazine or cutting ribbons and declaring buildings open. What a waste of time – not to mention ribbon. 'No, thank you very much,' she thought. 'Being a princess sounds absolutely rubbish. When I grow up, I'm going to be Chancellor of the Exchequer'.[2]

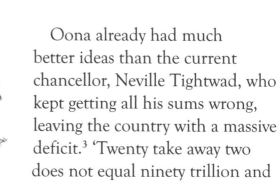

Oona already had much better ideas than the current chancellor, Neville Tightwad, who kept getting all his sums wrong, leaving the country with a massive deficit.[3] 'Twenty take away two does not equal ninety trillion and

[2]  The person in charge of all the money and sums for the whole country.
[3]  When the country owes lots of money.

three,' sighed Oona as Mr Tightwad announced the figures in his latest budget.[4] But her father, the king, wouldn't hear a word of it. 'Being Chancellor of the Exchequer is far too difficult a job for a girl,' he snapped. 'Princesses can't solve equations or do algebra.[5] Tell you what, here's a grand[6] – go and buy yourself a sparkly new tiara.'

One day, while the king was busy posing for his official royal portrait, Oona sneaked into his counting house and counted all his money. She spent all day doing the sums to calculate exactly how much cash was needed to pay the country's bills. (She also calculated that it took her three quills, eleven inkpots and 322 sheets of paper to do these sums, but that's beside the point.) Just as she was on the brink of saving the entire kingdom three hundred and fifty million pounds a week, a voice boomed out from behind her: 'Oona, dear, does my bottom look big in this?'

---

[4] A plan to make sure you always have enough money.
[5] A sort of maths involving letters as well as numbers.
[6] A thousand pounds.

The king was standing in the doorway, clutching a rather unflattering portrait under his arm. When he saw Oona's sums spread out all over the floor, his face turned so purple that Oona was worried the portrait artist would have to completely redo the painting. 'Enough is enough, young lady!' boomed the beetroot-faced king. 'This is the final straw! I'm hiring you a royal tutor! You are going to learn all the things that princesses ought to learn, like waving nicely and smiling and sewing and receiving floral bouquets and cutting ribbons and walking elegantly on ten-inch-high heels. *Not* doing complex calculations!'

'But that's not fair!' cried Oona, tears stinging her eyes.

'And I'm banning counting throughout the kingdom just to make a point!' declared the king. 'It will be high treason, punishable by three hundred years in prison!'

So Ms Phyllis Snootfest was hired after she spotted a job advertisement for 'the most boring princessing tutor in the land'. Every morning, afternoon and night, Ms Snootfest would force Oona to do silly exercises like walking on cobbles in glass slippers with the entire

*Encyclopedia Britannica*[7] balanced on her head to maintain perfect princess posture. Oona didn't want to carry the books on her head; she wanted to read them (even though she had already read every volume twenty times and was currently in the middle of writing an early version of Wikipedia.)[8]

Oona's despair had almost reached boiling point[9] when she conjured up a cunning plan from thin air, the way geniuses generally do. She remembered a bedtime story the king had once told her about a princess who pricked her finger on a spinning wheel and fell asleep for a hundred years. She decided she would pretend to do the exact same thing during her own sewing lesson! That way, Oona would be able to sneak into the counting house at night while everyone else was asleep and do as many sums as she liked without being sentenced to 300 years in prison. Oona was delighted with her cunning plan and set about putting it into action by pinching a bottle of fake blood from the royal jester's quarters and practising her pretend snoring.

Oona was all set for the big day when troubling news reached the palace: nobody in the kingdom was able to get to sleep, no matter how hard they tried. Lying down didn't work. Closing their eyes didn't work. Comfy pillows didn't make the slightest bit of difference. Everybody in the kingdom was wandering around in their pyjamas, yawning and baggy-eyed. Even Phyllis Snootfest couldn't doze off, and she usually bored herself to sleep.

---

[7]  About thirty large books crammed full of general knowledge.

[8]  A similar thing to the *Encyclopedia Britannica*, but much bigger and on the internet, which hadn't even been invented yet.

[9]  Usually the temperature at which a liquid becomes a gas but, in this case, it means the point at which Oona could bear it no longer.

The king was so tired that he didn't have the energy to fathom the answer to such a complex problem. He decided to sleep on it – but of course he couldn't. Oona – being a genius – took all of three minutes to work out what was going on. (Well, thirty seconds, actually, but it took two minutes to sneak the bottle of fake blood back to the jester's quarters and half a minute to get the king's attention.) 'Daddy, I know the answer!'

The king rolled his baggy eyes. 'Don't be ridiculous, Oona! Why would a little girl know the answer to anything? Don't bother me again until I've sorted out this blasted situation,' he yelled (through a yawn).

A day went by. And another. And another. Until eventually no one in the entire kingdom had slept for a hundred days.

Oona was extremely tired too. She was even more tired than the time a pea rolled under her extra thick, duck-feather-lined memory-foam mattress, causing her to toss and turn all night long. She was even more tired than the time she woke up from a nightmare in which she'd kissed her pet frog Ribbit and to her absolute horror he turned into a prince! But, most of all, she was tired of the king not listening to her.

Things in the kingdom had gone from terrible to terrible-er.

The sleep-deprived chancellor, Neville Tightwad, was making more mistakes than ever and the kingdom was quickly running out of cash. The king knew it was time to sort out this insomnia[10] inducing situation once and for all. But maybe just after he'd had a little nap . . . 'Oh dear,' sighed the king when he remembered he couldn't nap. 'I can't even manage one wink, never mind forty of the blighters.'

The king summoned the royal astronomer to look into the stars to see if he could find an answer . . . but all he could find were stars. If only he'd spotted a shooting star, he could have made a wish that people would sleep again. But, alas, he did not. Useless.

The king then summoned the chief royal scientist to do an experiment and . . . it worked! The king jumped for joy! The chief royal scientist jumped for joy! Everyone jumped for joy! And then they realised that the experiment had nothing to do with sleeping, and just proved that copper wire burns with a bright blue-green flame. Useless.

So the king summoned the royal jester, who told a joke. 'What do you call an Italian with a rubber toe?' the jester asked. 'Roberto!' he cried in an Italian accent. 'Get it? Rubber toe! Roberto! Ha ha ha ha!' Nobody laughed. Except the jester. Perhaps they were too tired or perhaps it was just a bad joke. Either way – useless.

The king's despair had now reached boiling point.[11] Exhausted, a laughing stock and a broken man, the king summoned Oona to ask for her help. 'You see, Daddy, it's really quite simple,' said Oona faster than the speed of light.[12] 'When you banned counting, nobody could count sheep to get to sleep, so that's why everyone is so tired.' Oona tried very hard not to look too pleased with herself, but she couldn't help but smile.

'Oh,' said the king. 'That really was quite simple.

---

[11] Remember? Usually the temperature at which a liquid becomes a gas, but, in this case, the point at which the King could bear it no longer.

[12] The fastest speed possible in the entire universe (30,000,000 metres per second).

So at last the problem was solved. The king lifted the counting ban, the nation took a very long nap and Oona was voted number-one top princess of all time by *Vanity Fairy Tale* magazine. All the eligible suitors in the kingdom queued up to meet her, but she didn't have time for suitors – she had much too much studying to do. Plus, Ribbit wanted to play leapfrog.

The king apologised to his daughter. 'I've been a bad king and a bad father. From now on you can use the counting house whenever you need peace and quiet to do your sums.' He then ordered the chief royal scientist to invent the calculator to help Neville Tightwad with his sums. He ordered the royal cook to prepare a celebratory feast, including a generous serving of humble pie[13] for His Majesty. And finally he ordered the royal jester to stop telling bad jokes. The celebrations continued till the stars came out and at last everyone fell asleep. Ahh! Finally!

Years later, when Oona was a grown-up, she became the first ever woman to be appointed Chancellor of the Exchequer. On day one in the job Oona decreed that maths and science would both be compulsory subjects in the national curriculum[14] for all primary school children. Oona became the country's most successful chancellor in history, turning Neville Tightwad's mess into a prospering economy.[15]

Oona also went on to improve upon the chief royal scientist's calculator by inventing the computer.[16] And then the internet. And then her favourite website, Wikipedia, which, you may remember, she had started writing when she was just a young princess.

'Ah,' sighed Oona, as she finally put her feet up. 'All in a good nine thousand six hundred and eighteen days' work.'

---

13  That's the pie you eat when you're sorry.
14  The list of what children in a kingdom should study.
15  When the country has lots of money and a bright future.
16  In the real world, the first person to realise that calculators were capable of so much more than just number crunching was a very clever woman called Ada Lovelace. Today over three billion people use computers and the internet, and half of them are women.

# Mouldysocks
# and the Three Bears

Mouldysocks was the messiest little boy in the world. In fact, if you weren't concentrating, you'd be forgiven for mistaking his bedroom for a rubbish tip. The floor was covered in old banana skins and stale sandwich crusts, with a load of rotten old apple cores and sticky sweet wrappers dotted around. Mouldysocks's toys were strewn all over the bed, and in the corner of the room festered a massive mound of multicoloured socks covered in multicoloured mould . . . hence the name Mouldysocks. The pong was so pungent that it made even poo smell nice!

The reason Mouldysocks was so messy was that he simply didn't have time to do *any* tidying up. He was far too busy playing computer games. He played *Candy Crunch* as he crunched his cornflakes, *Minedaft* on his way to school and the millisecond he got home he always liked a game of *Mario Fart*.

One day, Mouldysocks's mum asked him to go to the shops to buy a bottle of Sugar and Spice and All Things Nice air freshener to de-stink the house, which now smelt as bad as sweaty, cheesy feet. Gross!

'Ugh! Do I have to?' complained Mouldysocks. 'I'm in the middle of *Mario Fart*! I've nearly collected a hundred gold farts – I'll get an extra life soon . . .'

'But your room smells worse than a skunk who's swum in a sewer!' yelled Mrs Socks.

Mouldysocks grudgingly paused his game of *Mario Fart* and stomped out of the house. Luckily for him, he had taken his germ-covered electronic tablet with him so he could keep playing games on his way to the shops. Unluckily for him, he was so busy concentrating on a particularly problematic level of *Candy Crunch* that he immediately took a wrong turn. Instead of taking the path signposted To The Lovely Safe Shops, he accidentally took the path signposted To The Very Dangerous, Very Spooky, Very Scary Forest.

'Oh dear,' thought Mouldysocks when he next looked up several hours later. 'I must have taken a wrong turn. This forest seems very dangerous, very spooky and very scary, and now it's very dark too. Worst of all, my battery's only on ten per cent.'

Just as Mouldysocks thought it was game over, he spotted a faint light in the distance coming from a little cottage that was surrounded by trees, as things tend to be in forests.

'Phew!' he thought. 'I bet they'll have a charger!'

So Mouldysocks turned left past some trees, right past some more trees and left again past some other trees before finally arriving at the front door (which was next to a tree). Fortunately, the door was ajar (*not the type with jam in – it just means it was slightly open*) and Mouldysocks sauntered inside, all the while tapping away on his tablet.

The house was warm and inviting and, best of all, plugged into the wall was a charger. As he juiced up on battery power, Mouldysocks got a whiff of the most delicious scent, which cut through even the pungent pong of his socks. There, on the kitchen table, were three bowls of hot porridge and honey. His stomach growled like an angry bear. He'd never smelt such yummy food before – at home the smell of his socks usually overpowered everything else. He hadn't eaten a thing all day, so he tucked right in. The first bowl was far too hot and almost burnt his tongue. The second bowl was far too cold and almost gave his tongue frostbite. The third bowl, however, was *just right*, so Mouldysocks slurped it down in one go.

Unfortunately, he hadn't put his tablet down, and because it was still plugged into the wall, the cable got caught up with the table leg, which sent all three bowls flying, shattering and splattering porridge everywhere. 'Oh dear,' thought Mouldysocks.

Mouldysocks decided he deserved a rest after all this shattering and splattering, so he looked around for a chair.

The first chair he found was far too hard and completely covered in porridge. It made his bottom all achy and soggy.

The second chair was far too soft. It made him feel like he didn't even have a bottom, never mind a soggy one.

The third chair, however, was *just right*, so Mouldysocks decided to put his feet up. But he was so busy tapping away on his tablet that he didn't notice the chair leg slipping on a slick of porridge, and before he knew it the chair had toppled over, breaking into 55,555 porridge-soaked splinters.

'Oh dear,' thought Mouldysocks, surveying the carnage, 'it's getting a little messy down here. I think I'll go upstairs for a lie-down . . .'

Mouldysocks climbed the stairs to the bedroom, where he came across three beds. The first bed was far too high and he couldn't clamber onto it while still clutching on to his tablet. The second bed was far too far from the plug socket in case he needed to charge up more. The third bed, however, was *just right* (in both height and proximity to the plug socket) so Mouldysocks hopped on and curled up under the duvet to continue his game of *Candy Crunch*.

He was now on the brink of reaching Level 1,000, which nobody had ever managed before. Mouldysocks was concentrating so hard that his brain hurt, and his fingers were tapping so quickly you could hardly see them. Nearly . . . just one more piece of candy to crunch and . . . YES! He'd finally made it to level 1,000! Mouldysocks jumped up and down on the bed in delight but then . . .
CRRRRRRRAAAAASSSSSSSHHHHHHHHHHH!

The bed fell through the ceiling and landed with a thud in the kitchen below, causing complete and utter devastation. The room was now even messier than Mouldysocks's own bedroom – which, as you know, was very messy indeed. Not only were the walls covered in porridge but the floor was now covered in ceiling.

At the very same moment . . .
CRRREEEEEAAAAAAAAAAK!

The door opened and three bears appeared in the porch: Mummy Bear, Other Mummy Bear and their little baby bear.

'Hello there . . .' said Mouldysocks sheepishly, looking up from his tablet for the first time all day. 'Welcome home . . .?'

Mummy Bear and Other Mummy Bear were so upset at the state of their house that they both began to cry.

'What have you done to our lovely home?' wailed Mummy Bear.

'What are we going to eat? Where are we going to sit? And how are we going to sleep?' howled Other Mummy Bear, her big bear eyes crying big bear tears.

'And what's that awful smell putting me off my porridge?' whimpered Baby Bear.

'I'm so sorry!' said Mouldysocks. 'This is all my fault! I spent the entire day gaming and got myself lost, splattered your porridge, shattered your chair and battered your bedroom. I'm never using my tablet ever again!'

Yes, you heard him right! For the first time in his lazy life Mouldysocks willingly put down his tablet, picked up a bottle of mild green Beary Liquid and started to clean. He hoovered the hallway, dusted the drapes, polished the porcelain, and even replastered the ceiling.

When he had finished the house was spotless and the three bears gave him a huge bear hug.

'Wow! The house is cleaner than when we left it! said Mummy Bear.

'I should really be getting home now,' said Mouldysocks. 'My mum will be worried. The only thing is, I don't know the way . . .'

'Just use the GPS directions on your tablet,' said Other Mummy Bear, smiling. 'This forest has free Wi-Fi, so you'll be home in no time.'

'**Nooooo, not my tablet!**' cried Mouldysocks,
(*Unbelievable, I know, but that's what he said!*)

'It's fine to have a *bit* of screen time,' said Mummy Bear. 'We let Baby Bear have half an hour every day.'

'OK!' said Mouldysocks, switching it on.

'And, before you go, please take this with you,' said Mummy Bear, thrusting a bottle of Sugar and Spice and All Things Nice air freshener into his hands.

'Oh, and you might want these too,' said Other Mummy Bear, passing him a brand-new pair of socks. 'They smell of roses and posies rather than rotten eggs and pig poop.'

'Thank you,' said Mouldysocks, and suddenly his nose and head felt clearer than ever before.

'Where on earth have you been?' said his mum when he finally arrived home, 'I thought you'd been eaten alive by bears!'

'Don't be silly, Mum,' replied Mouldysocks. 'Bears don't eat boys. They eat honey porridge!'

'Hmm. Well, I hope you remembered the Sugar and Spice and All Things Nice air freshener. This house is stinkier than a big bear's bare backside.'

'If only she knew,' thought Mouldysocks, smiling to himself. He got to work on his bedroom straight away and in a matter of hours it was the cleanest room you've ever seen. No crumbs on the carpet, no stains on the surfaces and, best of all, no more mouldy socks. And he kept it that way. From that day on, Mouldysocks was a changed boy - he only used his tablet for half an hour a day (and that was mostly to order cleaning products online) and he regularly tidied up his room. He became so clean, in fact, that everyone had to stop calling him Mouldysocks. Brian was the happiest he'd ever been.

# Rap-Unzel

From the day she was born Rapunzel had extremely long hair. The midwives had never seen a baby like her. Her hair was longer than spaghetti, longer than a stretched-out slinky, even longer than a piece of string (however long that is). No matter how often her parents cut it, Rapunzel's hair would always grow back longer than before.

By the age of six her hair was so long she could use it as a skipping rope. By seven she could use it as a lasso. By eight she could use it as a picnic rug, although it was quite annoying when people dropped crumbs or spilled their milkshakes on it. And by the time she was nine years old, Rapunzel's hair was so long that it reached from her bedroom window right down to the street below. When she was grounded, her friends could climb up it and hang out without her parents knowing. Rapunzel loved her hair dearly and didn't know what she would do without it.

The other love of Rapunzel's life was musical poetry. She loved rap so much that at an early age she decided to change her name to **Rap**unzel. (Her parents had originally named her Unzel, but she always thought that sounded absolutely ridiculous.) With her awesome new name and even awesome-er hair, all Rapunzel wanted to do was spread her messages to the world through music.

One night while watching TV, Rapunzel's parents saw an advert for *Kingdom's Got Talent*, the TV show that searches for the kingdom's next great star. It gave them an idea. You see, they had wanted a baby so much but thought they could never have one, so when Rapunzel was born they vowed to give her every opportunity in life they could.

When she was just six months old, Rapunzel's parents had entered her into a beautiful baby contest but she was disqualified as the judges mistook her for a Yorkshire Terrier. As a toddler, they sent her to ballet classes but she was booted out because all the other children kept tripping up over her extra-long locks. When she was a little girl, they got her music lessons but her hair kept getting tangled in the trombone. However, Rapunzel never gave up on her rapping, so when her parents saw the advert for *Kingdom's Got Talent* they insisted she apply.

After weeks of rehearsing, the day of the auditions finally came around. Rapunzel's mum gave her a huge hug.

'At last you'll be able to get your music out there!' she said proudly.

'**Good luck, Unzel!**' her dad cried. Rapunzel winced as she left the house – she hated that name!

When Rapunzel arrived at the auditions, she couldn't believe the size of the queue. It was almost as long as her locks! Surely she didn't have the slightest chance against all these other people? But just as Rapunzel was about to give up and go home, an official-looking woman with a clipboard slapped a *KGT* sticker on her. 'Wow! Number 736! That's my lucky number!' thought Rapunzel. 'Maybe I do stand a chance after all!'

KGT
AUDITIONS

After another nine and a half hours of queueing, Rapunzel finally made it into the audition room.

'Unzel, is it? said the first judge, consulting her notes. 'Bit of a weird name. What's your talent, Unzel?'

'It's Rapunzel, actually, and I love to rap about my life. I want to get my messages out to the world.'

'So does everyone,' said Simon Scowl, the head judge, sounding bored and raising his eyes so high that everyone could see his nostril hair.

'Yes, I know!' blurted out Rapunzel defensively. 'But my parents had a really hard time having a baby and I just want to make them proud. You see, my mum ate some herbs because she was having pregnancy cravings but it turned out they were from a witch's garden and then the witch wanted to take me away when I was born, so we had to move house and . . .'

'Yeah, yeah, great backstory,' said Simon Scowl, yawning. 'Would make a charming fairy tale, I'm sure. OK, Rapunzel, off you go.'

Rapunzel stepped forward and cleared her throat. Suddenly, all her confidence disappeared as she became aware of a thousand eyes staring at her from the audience. There was absolute silence in the auditorium. You could literally hear a pin drop.

'Sorry! That was me!' said the first judge, picking up a pin she had just dropped.

'This song is all about sharing,' said Rapunzel uncertainly.

'*My ice cream*
*Brings all my friends to my place*
*And they say it's really ace*
*Have some*
*It's really nice*
*Try some*
*Take my advice*

*Sharing is caring*
*It's very kind.*
*Sharing is caring*
*It's good you'll find*

*My ice cream*
*Brings all my friends round mine*
*Try some*
*It's so sublime*

27

*Have some*
*We can share*
*Eat it*
*It's over there*

*Sharing is caring*
*Let's eat ice cream.*
*Sharing is caring*
*Know what I mean'*

There was total silence . . .
And then . . .

. . . the judges leapt to their feet, whooping and clapping. 'That
was PHENOMENAL!' exclaimed the first judge.

'Yeah, not bad,' said Simon Scowl. 'But I gotta ask, why all the hair?'

'Errr . . . it's my, err . . . hair,' answered Rapunzel. 'And I like it.'

'Well, I can't say that I do,' replied Simon Scowl, 'but your rapping
isn't the worst thing I've ever heard – that much I *can* say. NEXT!'

Rapunzel couldn't sleep all the following week. Even using her
hair as an eye mask didn't help. Would she get through to the next
round? There was so much competition. The judges had seen 735 acts
before her, including a princess who could multiply ten-digit numbers
together in her head, a boy who could turn baked beans into a super-
high beanstalk, and a gingerbread kid who told baking-based jokes.

She rifled through the post every day, hoping for good news, but all that came through the letterbox were electricity bills or take-away menus that went straight into the recycling bin (except the menu for Ali Baba's new kebab shop, that is, because there was a voucher attached for 'forty per cent off').

Finally, one day, a golden envelope dropped through the letterbox. The envelope was sealed with a wax outline of Simon Scowl's frowny face. Rapunzel ripped it open so quickly she almost tore the letter inside. The letter informed her that her *Kingdom's Got Talent* audition

had been successful and she'd made it through to the live televised final! At last she could get her music out to the masses! Rapunzel was over the moon! Until she read the small print, that was. ALWAYS read the small print. (If Rapunzel read the small print more often she would have realised that the 'forty per cent off' deal at Ali Baba's was on a minimum spend of £5,000.) In teeny-weeny writing, the size of specks of fairy dust, the small print of the *KGT* letter read:

PS Before you can appear on our extremely popular television show, you must lose at least three pounds in weight because the camera adds eight. You'll have to get a fake tan as the studio lights will make you look pale, and your teeth will need to be whitened so mine don't look too bright in comparison. Oh, and I almost forgot, you'll have to cut off all your hair as it looks really, really stupid.
Yours grouchily, Simon Scowl.

The very next day, Rapunzel trudged to the hairdressers, her long hair trailing slowly behind her. She slumped down in the salon chair and took one last look at her luxurious locks. A solitary tear trickled down her face as she remembered all the good times they'd had together.

Just as the hairdresser was about to cut her hair, Rapunzel jumped to her feet and bolted out of the door, her precious curls still firmly attached to her noggin. She knew that raw emotion like this always resulted in her best work and she immediately began channelling her anger into her lyrics.

VIEWS

That evening, Rapunzel uploaded her brand-new rap video 'Be Who You Are' to the internet and within minutes she had notched up over ten billion views.

Overnight, Rapunzel became a viral sensation. Her phone wouldn't stop ringing! Requests flooded in for her to appear in shampoo adverts, along with offers of her own hair-clip range! She was even asked to compose the theme music for the next Bond movie! One particular request caught Rapunzel's eye: *Kingdom's Got Talent* had asked her to appear as the star act in the final now that she was famous. They even said she could keep her hair 'if she must'. Rapunzel refused their offer point-blank. She decided to accept a different offer from a rival TV channel instead to perform a live outdoor charity concert on the same night. The concert was a total sell-out and the following week *Kingdom's Got Talent* was cancelled because of its low ratings. Rapunzel announced a world tour with all profits going to a hair-loss charity and from then on never a day went by that she didn't appreciate how lucky she was to have hair like hers . . . even if it did occasionally get tangled up in her shoelaces.

'Be who you are
And are who you be
Won't change the way I look
I just wanna be me

Like who I am
I can't change for you
I'll be who I am
I just gotta stay true

Don't care if you stare
I won't cut my hair
I like who I am
(Beat) So there
You be you
And I'll be me
Won't change the way I look
So leave me be

No one should change you
Or rearrange you
Be true to yourself
And just love the strange you

Be who you are
And are who you be
Won't change the way I look
I just wanna be me'

# TRUMPLESTILTSKIN

In a faraway land called the United States of Kraziness (or USK for short) there once lived an angry little man with a fuzzy orange hairpiece and a funny orange face. Although nobody knew his real name, he was nicknamed Trumple. Everyone thought that Trumple had been given his nickname because ever since he was a tiny baby he couldn't stop 'trumping' or breaking wind. He pretty much farted ALL THE TIME. The problem had only worsened as he grew older because of his terrible diet of junk food and fizzy drinks. All the colouring and additives had turned both him and his weird wig bright orange – so much so that he was almost fluorescent.

If there was one thing Trumple loved as much as himself it was gold. As a baby he wore gold nappies, sucked on a gold dummy and rattled a gold rattle whenever he was rattled. The older he got, the more and more gold he wanted. Oh, and power – he wanted more and more of that too. So as soon as he was old enough he joined the family business, grabbing himself more and more gold and more and more power, until he was completely in charge. But even that wasn't enough. Nothing was enough for Trumple. Not the skyscrapers he now owned, nor the companies he now ran, nor the hotels and golf courses he had acquired, not even the fact he lived in a giant golden tower called Trumple Tower – oh no . . . none of it was enough – he still wanted more. Trumple wanted to be king!

The USK already had a king who was kind and caring, but Trumple wasn't going to let a silly little detail like that get in his way.

'I want to be king!' he yelled from his golden high chair, throwing a tantrum and throwing the king and his daughter Marla into the palace's deepest dungeon. It was a dark, dingy dungeon, with the tiniest little window so high up that you couldn't even see out of it.

Trumple instantly set about redecorating the palace in his favourite colour. Yes, you guessed it: gold. And not just painted with gold-coloured paint – he wanted the real deal. Everything was to be

pure gold. He wanted 900 golden mirrors – at least one in every room – so he could look at himself all day long. He wanted to replace his normal-sized hairpiece with the biggest golden hairpiece in the kingdom. He even wanted a golden toilet to trump and do his business on (the toilet variety *and* the striking deals variety).

Before long the kingdom was running out of gold. The goldmines were empty and the people were struggling to keep up with Trumple's increasing demands. Everyone in the kingdom had given him their gold, and they were now poor and hungry and without proper healthcare. (He had sold off the healthcare system in exchange for yet more gold!) But Trumple wasn't content because the palace still wasn't covered entirely in gold. He banged his tiny hands on his half-gold table in a fit of fury.

**'I want gold everywhere,'** he screamed. **'I want it everywhere – NOW!!!'**

Trumple turned such a luminous shade of tangerine that his advisers had to shield their eyes. Just as he was about to throw all his toys out of the pram, so to speak, one of his terrified aides piped up: 'I think the old king's daughter can spin straw into gold, your royal orange-ness.'

Immediately Trumple ordered Princess Marla to spin all the straw in the kingdom into gold. But Marla was an intelligent and stubborn young girl, and, knowing she could strike a better deal, she refused. So Trumple made Marla an offer: if she spun ten kilometres of straw into gold, he would give her three chances to guess his real name, and if she guessed it correctly, he would free her and her father from the dungeons. As it was her only hope, Marla agreed. She spun and spun and spun until her fingers were red and raw and the entire palace was finally covered in gold. The household was so shiny and blinging that nobody could see where they were going. The servants kept getting dazzled and were constantly bumping into each other.

Meanwhile Marla was at her wits' end: she just couldn't guess Trumple's real name. She'd already had two really good guesses but it turned out that Trumple wasn't actually called Poopoohead or Fartyfartybumpants and now the time was fast approaching for her final guess. Marla's dad, the wise old king, had pondered the problem long and hard and suggested that perhaps Trumple was short for something. But what?

Trumpleton?
Trumplesmith?
Trumplepoopoohead?
Trumplefartyfartybumpants?

It was no use. All was lost. Marla stared forlornly into one of the golden mirrors Trumple had left in the dungeons so he could gaze at himself when he came to taunt the old king. As she watched a tear roll down her cheek, Marla spotted something in the corner of the mirror. Reflected through the bars of her cell window, she could just about make out a huge gold sign being hung by workmen over the palace gates.

'NIKSTLITSELPMURT,' it read.

'Nikstlitselpmurt!' thought Marla, 'could that be Trumple's real name?' It would certainly make sense for a person as self-obsessed as Trumple to have his name emblazoned in gold across the front of his palace. But she had never heard of anybody called Nikstlitselpmurt before.

Marla pondered this strange word for a moment. But only for a moment.

'I've got it!' she cried. 'We're reading the word in a mirror. If you look at any word in a mirror, it will be spelt back to front. All we need to do is read the word backwards! Nikstlitselpmurt backwards is Trumplestiltskin! Trumplestiltskin, that's his real name!'

Marla and the king hugged each other and cried tears of happiness. They would finally be free!

When they told Trumplestiltskin his name, he was furious. He couldn't believe they had worked it out locked away in the dungeon without newspapers or social media! How had they known? He just couldn't understand it.

'Not fair!' he cried, kicking and screaming and spilling his milk everywhere.

The orange colour in his face had reached nuclear levels and it seemed as though his entire head might explode.

**'Noooooooooooooooooooooooo!!!'** he cried as he let out a trump so terrific that the whole palace shook. It was the loudest fart Marla had ever heard. It was so forceful, in fact, that it sent Trumplestiltskin flying into space – never to be seen again.

*Postscript:*
Marla is currently studying International Relations at a world-class university, while her father enjoys a successful career on the after-dinner speaking circuit and has his own TV series on Netflix.

# Trumplestiltskin

# Lil' Red Riding in the Hood

Lil' Red Riding was an up-and-coming fashion designer, well known in her neighbourhood. Locals loved wearing her outfits and when she first launched her signature Lil' Red Riding Hoodies they sold out instantly. The hoodies, inspired by a hooded cloak that her grandmother had made for her, came in a variety of different colours, but were especially popular in red.

Red lived on the Rough Estate with her mum and dad, Mr and Mrs Riding. People often referred to the estate as 'the hood' because calling it the Rough Estate made it sound like an undesirable place to live, when, in fact, it had been named after Ernest Rough, the

44

world-famous architect who had designed it. Red loved the estate; it was lively and crammed full of characters from all different walks of life. Granny Riding had lived there ever since it was built in the 1960s. She had even met Ernest Rough once.

Although she loved seeing her friends and neighbours wearing her designs, Red wanted the whole world to wear her clothes – 'A tricky feat for a little girl from the hood,' her granny would say, 'but if anyone can do it, you can.' Red knew that to really hit the big time she would need to design something extra eye-catching for her spring/summer catwalk collection at the forthcoming Fairy Tale Fashion Week. Something with the 'wow' factor. Unfortunately, she was all out of ideas and for the last few days she had been driving herself crazy trying to figure out what to make. A wolf-wool waistcoat? Chainmail undies? Glass pyjamas with matching glass slippers?

To make matters worse, Red also had her granny to worry about. Granny Riding had put her back out after a rather nasty weight-lifting injury and was unable to get out of bed. Red decided to bring over some home-baked gingerbread men to cheer her up.

Red loved visiting Granny, who was by far the most fascinating person she knew. She often recounted tales from the olden days about men she had kissed who had turned out to be frogs and other men she had kissed who had turned out to be toads. But Red especially loved hearing about how fashion was back then: the shift dresses in the 60s, kaftans in the 70s, shoulders pads in the 80s, combat trousers in the 90s and a whole host of other inspirational designs in between and beyond. Granny Riding had the most stylish wardrobe of vintage clothes Red had ever seen – yet another inspiration for Red's rad designs.

'Be careful when walking through the hood,' Mrs Riding called out as Red was putting her cloak on. 'I don't want you getting caught up in any trouble.'

'Don't worry about me, Mum,' Red replied. 'I can take care of myself.'

As she made her way across the Rough Estate, Red spotted a stylish girl in a vintage tea dress and super-cool cowboy boots topped off with one of Red's trademark hoodies. Red smiled to herself – another happy customer! But as she got closer Red realised that a bully was throwing sticks and stones at the girl.

'Hey!' shouted Red. 'Stop that right now or you'll break her bones!'

The bully ran off before Red could give them a proper piece of her mind.

Red approached the girl, who was clearly shaken up, and as she got closer she realised it wasn't a girl at all – it was a boy.

'Hey! I love your outfit!' said Red.

'Thanks!' said the boy, instantly starstruck at the sight of Lil' Red Riding. 'I'm Wülf. I'm a massive fan of your clothes. I have your hoodies in every colour, including the limited-edition "woodcutter" design. That's my favourite!'

'Thanks!' said Red. 'The image of the woodcutter symbolises strength and drive. Sometimes the axe feels heavy but the woodcutter has to keep chopping or there'll be no firewood – I guess that's how life can be sometimes.'

'That's so cool,' said Wülf. 'Everything you say is so cool! I read that interview you did with *Vague* magazine. You're really talented.'

47

'I don't feel so talented at the moment,' said Red. 'I can't seem to come up with anything for my upcoming show at Fashion Week.'

'Think woodcutter,' said Wülf. 'You've totally got the drive and strength to work it out.'

'Enough about me,' said Red. 'Are you OK? Why don't you come with me to my granny's for a cup of tea and a gingerbread man? She used to be a doctor – she can take a look at those nasty grazes for you.'

As Granny tended to his cuts and bruises, Wülf explained just how much he loved women's fashion, but how he kept getting bullied for wearing it. Granny listened intently.

'You must be roasting under that big duvet, Granny,' said Red, pulling it back to reveal the intricately stitched nightie Granny was wearing. Red had designed it for her when she had become bedridden.

'WOW!!' said Wülf. 'I simply love that piece you're wearing. The craftsmanship is exquisite!'

'It's one of a collection,' said Red, pointing to the other nighties she had made for her granny.

'Red, these are mind-blowing!' shrieked Wülf with delight. 'I've never seen anything like it!'

'Try one on, my dear!' suggested Granny. 'It's such a shame no one ever gets to admire them. I don't get many visitors in my bedroom these days.'

Wülf didn't hesitate and immediately slipped one over his head. It looked stunning: sequins gleaming in among brightly coloured embroidery, all framed within immaculate tailoring. Then there was the

standout centre-piece: a beautifully hand-stitched sparkling outline of a woodcutter, sewn delicately in glistening silver thread. Wülf's eyes lit up. 'Red, you must show these nighties in your next catwalk show! You'll be the talk of the town!'

Granny's eyes lit up too. 'Yes, you must, Red! They'll be a huge hit!'

Now Red's eyes lit up. She'd had an idea. 'And *you* must model them, Wülf! They look incredible on you!'

Wülf could hardly believe his luck. He had never worn anything a thousandth as beautiful or artistic.

Weeks later, when Granny had fully recovered, she found herself in the front row of the spring/summer catwalk show at Fairy Tale Fashion Week. She was squashed between the fearsome editor of *Vague* magazine, Anna Winteriscoming, and Skinny Rake, the world's most famous catwalk model and the face of Sugar and Spice and All Things Nice perfume.

Granny tried to make conversation with Skinny but she was a girl of few words.

'What big eyes you have . . .' said Granny.

'All the better for modelling with,' replied Skinny.

'What big lips you have . . .' said Granny.

'All the better for modelling with,' replied Skinny.

'What big teeth you have . . .' said Granny.

'All the better for lucrative toothpaste endorsements,' replied Skinny.

'Lovely, dear,' said Granny.

The show was a MASSIVE success, and Red and Wülf received a huge standing ovation.

'I would like to dedicate this show to my granny, the inspiration behind all my clothes,' said Red over thunderous applause. And then it was Granny's turn to receive a standing ovation.

In the weeks that followed Wülf quickly became Britain's next top model, renowned for his nonconformist and authentic looks. Meanwhile, boys and girls across the globe began wearing Lil' Red Riding nighties, often teamed with their Lil' Red Riding hoodies! And no one was prouder than Granny when Red Riding was voted Fashion Designer of the Year by *Vague* magazine. Lil' Red Riding had become **BIG!**

# JACK AND THE BAKED BEANSTALK

Jack was completely obsessed with baked beans. He ate beans on toast for breakfast, baked bean sarnies for lunch and loved nothing more than baked bean soup for dinner (basically just baked beans with most of the beans taken out). It was mid-afternoon and Jack was microwaving himself a massive slice of baked bean pie with an extra-massive dollop of baked beans on the side as a light pre-teatime snack when he noticed that five of the beans had started glowing a strange neon-orange colour.

'That's weird,' said Jack, showing the beans to his grandad.

'They've gone off!' grunted his grandad, tossing the entire bowl out of the window. 'If you eat those, you'll be farting all night like that Trumplestiltskin chap . . . or your grandmother.'

That night when Jack went to bed he dreamt that he couldn't stop farting and that his farts chased him all the way down the street. Jack woke up hot, clammy and disturbed and headed downstairs to fix himself a midnight snack of baked bean

ice cream. As he slurped it down, he noticed something out of the kitchen window and just for a moment he thought he was still dreaming. Because right there, in the garden, was the biggest baked-beanstalk you've ever seen. Jack closed his eyes and pinched himself (a sure-fire way to check if you're dreaming) but, when he opened his eyes again, the baked-beanstalk was still there.

The slimy orange plant climbed all the way up into the sky, past the birds, past the clouds, even past the ozone layer (*which, if you don't know, is very high indeed and starts at ten kilometres from the ground*). Jack estimated that it was at least a thousand times taller than the tallest building in the known universe (*incidentally, the Burj Khalifa in Dubai is only 828 metres high*). And it was certainly covered in more tomato sauce than the Burj Khalifa!

Jack was rubbing his sleepy eyes when, without warning, a ginormous giant came hurtling down the beanstalk at 344 metres per second.

'Weeeeeeeeeeeeeeeeeeee!' screamed the giant excitedly like he was sliding down the world's longest waterslide. But Jack didn't hear it till after the event as the giant was travelling faster than the speed of sound (*which is 343 metres per second, by the way*).

The giant crash-landed in Jack's grandad's vegetable patch, crushing the cabbages, squashing the squashes, mashing the marrows and leaving a **huge** crater in his wake.

**BONK**. (*That was the delayed noise of him landing because he was travelling faster than the speed of sound, remember?*)

Jack pinched himself again. 'Ouch!' he yelped. He was definitely still awake.

'**FEE-FI-FO-F**—oh dear, I'm a bit hoarse. I smell the juice of tomato sauce,' coughed the giant, trying to clear his throat.

'That'll be all the screaming,' said Jack. 'And the tomato sauce is from the beanstalk. It's covered in the stuff.'

'And so am I,' grinned the giant, licking some sauce off his giant forefinger. 'Oh bother . . . I'm going to have to have this jacket dry-cleaned.'

'I'll stick it in the wash . . . if it will fit in our machine,' laughed Jack. 'I'm Jack, by the way. Who are you?'

'Hi, Jack, I'm Janusz. I'm a giant – although it's possible you guessed that already,' he giggled, pulling a stray carrot out of his ear. Jack giggled too.

'Beat my beetroots and pummel my parsnips, what on earth is going on here?' exclaimed Jack's grandad, as he came out through the back door. 'Why is there a bloomin' baked-beanstalk in my . . . Oh no! My allotment's been **annihilated!'**

'Sorry about that, sir!' piped up Janusz. 'I'm afraid I've got a little portly of late. Need to lay off the baked beans. I'm addicted.'

'Me too,' said Jack, grinning. 'Can't get enough of them!'

They giggled again as Jack's grandad noticed Janusz for the first time.

# 'ARRRRRRRGGGGGHHHHHHH!'

There's a giant in my garden!' he screamed, running off down the street in his pyjamas and slippers, clutching his hot-water bottle.

'Don't mind him,' said Jack. 'Just a bit of a shock to find a giant sitting on your celery in the middle of the night.'

'It seems very nice here,' said the giant, surveying the area. 'I think I'll go and tell my friends all about it.' And with that the giant clambered back up the baked-beanstalk and disappeared out of sight.

A few weeks later, hundreds of giants had climbed down the beanstalk and the crater in Jack's garden was almost the size of the Vredefort Dome (*the largest crater in the world, which is more than 300 kilometres wide*). Many of the giants decided to settle in the local area and look for employment. Janusz quickly found a job on a building site on account of his ability to bend steel girders as though they were pipe cleaners, and lift boulders with his little finger. Jack and Janusz became great friends and would often hang out together. They would giggle away over a BLT (beans, larger beans and tomato sauce) – whenever Janusz wasn't working long hours to earn enough money to support his family back home in Giantland.

But trouble was brewing. Some of the villagers had started complaining about the giants stealing their jobs, leaving huge footprints everywhere and speaking Giantish instead of English. Jack thought this was thoroughly unfair as the giants were doing jobs the villagers didn't want to do and Giantish *was* their mother tongue after all. He knew how hard Janusz and the other giants worked to make sure their

families didn't go hungry. Plus, it wasn't *their* fault they had big feet. 'I've got big ears,' thought Jack, 'and that's not *my* fault.'

And so the village council decided there should be a vote on whether or not to chop down the baked-beanstalk. If more than fifty per cent (*that's half*) of the village council (*that's twelve people*) raised their hands, then the beanstalk was a goner (*that's chopped down*). If not, it stayed. Janusz was very nervous about the vote so Jack went along too for moral support.

'Raise your hand if you agree that the baked-beanstalk should be chopped down,' croaked the wizened old leader of the council.

Jack crossed his fingers and counted the raised hands. **One . . . two . . . three . . . four . . . five . . . SIX! Only six!**

Hurrah, only half of the people had put their hands up. It was a fifty-fifty split and not enough to take any action. 'Phew! That was a close shave' thought Jack. But he thought it a little too soon because at that moment another hand slowly rose up in the air. And it wasn't any old hand; it was Jack's grandad's old hand.

'I count seven hands,' declared the crinkled old council leader. 'That's more than half. The baked-beanstalk will be chopped down at midnight tonight.'

'How could you, Grandad?' cried Jack.

'I'm sorry, Jack, but it's just too "gianty" around here these days. You'll understand when you're older.'

But Jack was sure that he would never understand. Janusz was the kindest person he'd ever met and life was so much better with him in it.

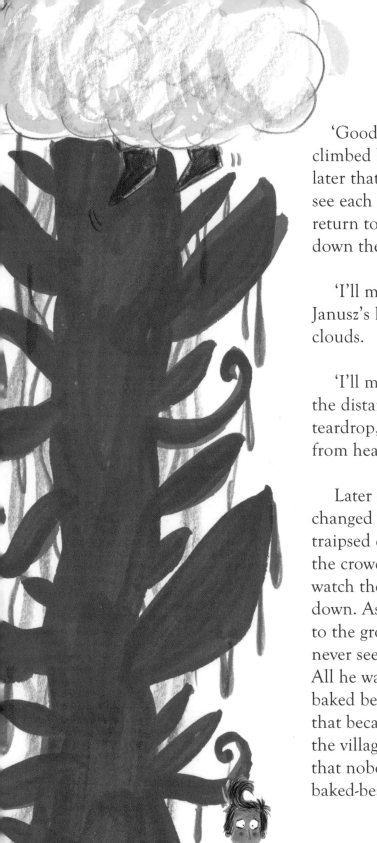

'Goodbye, Jack,' said Janusz, as he climbed back up the baked-beanstalk later that evening. 'I'm sorry we won't see each other again but I've got to return to my family before they chop down the beanstalk.'

'I'll miss you!' shouted Jack as Janusz's head disappeared into the clouds.

'I'll miss you too, Jack!' came the distant reply along with a giant teardrop, which soaked Jack through from head to toe.

Later that evening, after Jack had changed into some dry clothes, he traipsed down to the garden to join the crowd who had turned out to watch the beanstalk being chopped down. As the huge orange plant fell to the ground. Jack feared he would never see his best friend again. All he wanted to do was comfort-eat baked beans, but he couldn't even do that because all the baked beans in the village had been thrown away so that nobody could grow any more baked-beanstalks in the future.

In the weeks that followed the giants' departure, the villagers started to wonder if chopping down the beanstalk had been a terrible mistake. Because there were no giants left, there was nobody tall enough to change the light bulbs in lamp posts or to reach the high shelves in supermarkets or to build buildings quickly (the villagers took twice as long as the giants). But worst of all, the village felt a bit, you know, boring – full of the same boring people going about their same boring lives.

'I'm sorry, Jack,' said his grandad on the morning of Jack's tenth birthday. 'We should never have chopped down the beanstalk. Maybe you could wish for another beanstalk when you blow out your candles tonight.'

'Don't be silly, Grandad,' said Jack. 'Everyone knows wishes aren't real.'

'Nobody thought magic baked beans were real, dear boy,' replied his grandad. 'And just look how that turned out.'

That evening, as Jack blew out the candles on his baked-bean-shaped cake, he wished as hard as he could that another beanstalk would grow in the garden and that he would get to see his giant friend again. But nothing happened, so Jack sloped off to bed. It was the worst birthday **EVER**.

That night Jack just couldn't get to sleep. He tossed and turned and turned and tossed. No matter how many baked beans he counted, he simply couldn't drift off. As he rolled to the very edge of his bed, he suddenly became rather uncomfortable. It was almost as if there was something lodged between the bed frame and the mattress . . . something tin-shaped . . .

'Jumping jellybeans!' thought Jack. 'My emergency beans!' Jack had always kept a tin of emergency baked beans hidden under his mattress in case there was ever a national shortage. How could he have forgotten? He raced downstairs in his pyjamas, emptied the tin into a bowl and shoved it in the microwave.

## *PING!*

Jack pulled out the bowl. All the beans looked completely normal . . . except for five of them that were glowing a strange neon-orange colour and lighting up Jack's face, which had the biggest smile on it you've ever seen. A giant smile, you might say . . .

# THE PRINCESS AND THE SNOG

Did you ever hear tell of the stinky-breathed frog
Who was well known to dwell in the dingy old bog?
The locals and yokels always steered clear
Cos the stench of his breath made you faint when too near.

At the top of the hill, far away from the stink
Lived a cool little girl whose hair was bright pink.
Her name was Pandora; she just loved to box –
She owned a gold punchball for punches and knocks.

One day as she practised
her left and right hook
She hit it so hard that the
whole building shook.
The big golden ball snapped
off from her blow
And fell off its pole to the floor down below.

It rolled out her room and then out the front door
It rolled past the shops and then rolled a bit more
It rolled down a hill and bounced off a sheepdog
And into a field where it went on to leapfrog
The farmer, his wife and a
long row of sheep
Then the ball gathered pace
(as the field was so steep).

It sploshed in a spring and then boinged off a log,
And landed smack-bang in the dingy old bog.
Shoving pegs on her nostrils to stifle the stink
Pandora said, 'Yikes! My ball's going to sink!'
She ran to the edge of the dingy old bog,
Where she came face to face with the stinky-breathed frog.

He was holding her punchball between his webbed feet
With a slimy old smile that he thought looked quite sweet.
'Well, well,' croaked the frog, 'are you looking for this?
I'll give you the ball if you give me a kiss!'

'Please just pass it back,' she said, firm but polite
And hoped that the frog wouldn't put up a fight
But the frog was already applying his lipstick –
'Oh geez,' thought Pandora. 'This guy's such a dipstick.'

Pandora now pondered her current predicament.
Kissing a frog needs a willing participant
And given she didn't like stinky-breathed frogs
She certainly wouldn't be dishing out snogs!

But although she was
tough and an expert at
boxing,
Punching was wrong so
she'd have to outfox him.
'Pucker up,' said the frog,
'it's time for a smooch!
I've the lips of a camel and
breath of a pooch!'

'That's it!' thought Pandora,
as froggy edged in –
'My breath needs to smell
like a fishmonger's bin!'
So as frog puckered up with
a squish and a squelch
Pandora emitted the
world's biggest belch.

She almost passed out from the terrible pong
(The pegs barely helped – it was really that strong).
The frog took one whiff and fell back in the bog
And that was the end of the stinky-breathed frog.

The ball rolled straight over to Pandora's feet
As she popped in a mint to make her smell sweet.
'Well,' thought Pandora, 'that frog
was a schmuck!'
And she burped one more time –
you know, just for good luck.

So never kiss frogs unless it's
your wish,
And please if you do,
always know this . . .
A very wise rule for a
mister or miss:
You choose who you
hug and you choose
who you kiss.

# THE BOY WHO CRIED WOOL

Angora was an extremely sensitive toy – a knitted woollen boy, wise beyond his years. He knew that the world wasn't always a happy place and sometimes you had to go through hardship, but that you could learn from it and become a stronger person. Knowing this didn't always make it easier, though, and he often felt overwhelmed with emotion. He was the type of boy who would cry at the sad bits in movies, like when people waved goodbye to planes carrying away loved ones, when couples kissed in the pouring rain and when old ladies threw their necklaces into the ocean.

You see, Angora had been around for an awfully long time and had lived through a lot. At over a hundred years old he had first belonged to a little girl named Pearl, whose mum had made him during the First World War out of leftover wool. Volunteers had knitted extra clothes for the soldiers who were busy fighting, and Angora had been created for Pearl from the surplus wool of a lost officer's jumper.

Angora had seen many changes as he was passed down from generation to generation. Two world wars had been fought. Mobile phones and the internet had been invented and nearly all families had cars and TVs nowadays. When Angora was first knitted, most households didn't even

have a radio. He missed the old days dearly, but he enjoyed modern life too. The people he loved had come and gone, but every decade or so he found himself in the care of a new member of Pearl's family. These days he belonged to MJ.

From day one MJ was inseparable from Angora. He was by his side in the cot, in his arms as a toddler, in his bag during nursery and when MJ was big enough, in his bed every night. But as soon as MJ started school, Angora felt things begin to change. MJ started playing with new toys: toys that had batteries and could make noises, flash lights or play music. There were cars that drove, action figures that spoke, and even a fighter plane that flew. And MJ loved them all.

Soon Angora was no longer in MJ's bed but dumped at the bottom of the toy box. The very bottom.

It was dark, even in the daytime, and the conditions were cramped. Angora was squashed under several other toys, and was worried he'd get all tatty and torn. Angora was sadder than he'd ever been. He felt weak and tired, frayed and afraid. The wool around his eyes had begun to come loose and even though toys aren't supposed to cry, Angora did. He cried and cried and cried. The wool spooled from his eyes.

'What if I never get out of here? Or, worse still, what if I'm thrown away?' he thought to himself.

'Yo, wool-boy! Why are you crying?' asked a nearby T. rex. 'Boys aren't supposed to cry. Boys are supposed to scare people like I do. Watch this!'

The T. rex opened his gigantic jaws to reveal his terrifying razor-sharp teeth and roared at three passing clockwork mice. The mice squeaked at the top of their tiny lungs before scurrying out of sight on their tiny plastic wheels.

'But I don't want to scare people,' said Angora. 'That's a horrible thing to do.'

'Does. Not. Compute,' spluttered a large metallic robot who had overheard their conversation. 'Boys. Should. Be. Tough. And. As. Hard. As. Steel. Like. Me.'

'But I don't want to be as hard as steel,' said Angora. 'I'd rather be as soft as wool.'

'You don't want to listen to them wimps,' chipped in a toy soldier who was on patrol nearby. 'Real boys like breaking people's noses. Do you wanna fight me? Go on, stick 'em up!'

'No, thank you,' said Angora. 'I don't like fighting. Real boys don't fight. Real boys have feelings.'

'Pah! Suit yourself!' said the toy soldier. 'Then MJ will never play with you!'

'I hope that's not true,' said Angora sadly, as more loops of wool began coiling down his cheeks.

'Hey! Why don't you fight me?' said the toy soldier to the robot. 'I could knock your LED lights out!'

'Affirmative. Fight. Accepted,' replied the robot.

The toy soldier swung his sword so hard that it dented the robot's arm. What's more, his sword snapped clean off from where it had been glued into his hand.

'Oh no, my lovely sword!' wailed the soldier, trying very hard not to cry.

'I'm. Dented,' sobbed the robot, fighting back his tears. 'Must. Not. Cry.'

'But it's OK to cry,' said Angora. 'It can help you, I promise.' And with that, Angora took some woollen tears that had fallen from his eyes and made a sling to bandage up the robot's arm. He then took some more tears and tied the sword back into the soldier's hand.

'It sometimes helps to let it out – it makes you feel better. Crying can be the best medicine. Being tough isn't always the answer, you know.' Tears flooded down the robot's and the soldier's faces.

T. rex nodded. 'Us dinosaurs always had to fight to survive. But a fat lot of good that did us . . .' He sighed and tears rolled down his cheeks too.

Angora comforted his new friends and eventually they felt happier again.

Meanwhile, on the outside of the toy box, somebody else was sad. MJ was unwell. He had a high temperature and had been given medicine by the doctor. He felt so tired that he could hardly lift his head, and he'd even had to stay off school for two days. Nothing was making him feel better. None of his toys were helping – not the car that drove nor the fighter plane that flew, and he was too poorly to play-fight with his action figures. By the time his Grandpa Max came to visit, MJ was more upset than he'd ever been.

'It's OK to cry,' said Grandpa Max. And so MJ did. He cried and cried and cried, and Grandpa Max wiped away the salty tears streaming from MJ's eyes. 'Feeling rotten is rotten. It's OK to be upset, little soldier.'

Grandpa Max's words always made MJ feel better. His hugs helped a lot too.

'Sometimes crying is the best medicine,' said Grandpa Max, holding Max Junior tightly in his arms and, for the first time in days, MJ fell into a deep sleep. While MJ slept, Grandpa Max remembered his favourite toy as a child and went searching for him - eventually finding him at the bottom of the toy box. He picked Angora up, wiped away his woollen tears, and popped him into bed next to MJ, who cuddled Angora all night long. Angora cuddled MJ back and the next morning they both awoke feeling happier than ever.

From that day on MJ always kept Angora in his bed. Over the years they had many a cuddle and a cry together (often while watching an old movie) and they always felt stronger afterwards. They both knew that having a good cry was the best medicine to help sad thoughts melt away.

# Princess and The Peashooter

Zareen lived with her dad and his second wife, Tania, in the magical London suburb of Crystal Palace. It was magical because it was here she had first met her best friend, Yasmin, and here that her dad had first met Tania. Zareen loved her stepmother Tania to bits. She wasn't the sort of wicked stepmother that you read about in fairy tales; she was kind, thoughtful and extremely cool. She had very long nails, which she painted a different colour every day and she always called Zareen 'Princess'.

Zareen was pretty cool herself. She wore a sequinned headscarf, which Tania had bought her one Saturday at the Stressfield shopping centre. She was really into rap music and knew loads of lyrics, plus she was always the first to hear about the latest crazes. Recently she'd been collecting the highly sought-after *Fearless Fairy Tale Collectors' Cards*. She had Sleeping Brainy right through to Mouldysocks. The only card missing from her collection was Rapunzel, which was annoying because it was the one she wanted most of all.

There had been a whole load of new crazes at the school lately. For a while people had become obsessed with Zoom Frisbees (*basically just an overpriced cardboard circle*) and had spent all break time throwing them to each other in the playground. Next came Zoom Paper Aeroplanes (*basically just some overpriced folded-up paper*), which people had spent all lunchtime throwing to each other in the canteen. Then there were Zoomerangs (*basically just an overpriced cardboard V-shape*), which you could throw to yourself pretty much anywhere. One evening Zareen saw an advert on TV for a Zoom Peashooter (*basically just an overpriced paper straw*), which she was sure would be the next big thing. The ad featured a dancing pea who sang a song that was so catchy Zareen couldn't get it out of her head.

*'The cool kids, they love shooting peas,*
*And all you need is one of these,*
*So get down on your hands and knees and beg your parents:*
*Please, please, PLEASE!'*

'Please can I have one, Tania?' Zareen pleaded, although she didn't actually get down on her hands and knees.

'I'm not sure, Princess,' Tania replied. 'They seem a little dangerous and a bit expensive for a paper straw.'

'But everybody else's parents will get them one,' begged Zareen. 'And then I'll be the only kid in school without one. Pleeeeeassse can I have one? Pretty please topped with peas?'

'Oh, all right then,' said Tania, 'but I'm buying it online. There's no way I'm taking you to Stressfield at rush hour.'

The very next day Zareen's peashooter arrived in a shiny green box that said ZOOM PEASHOOTERS – BE THE COOLEST KID IN YOUR POD in large emerald letters on the front. Zareen gave Tania the hugest hug and rushed off to school to show all her friends.

Soon Zareen was the envy of the playground. She showed everyone how it worked: you inserted the pea into a tube-like device, blew a huge puff of air into one end and the pea shot out the other end at almost rocket speed (*that's 7.9 kilometres per second, or 1,764 m pea h*). Zareen shot pea after pea into the air and one even went so far it landed on the other side of the school gates. She was officially the coolest kid in school.

The following day, the peashooter craze had spread like crazy (*as crazes tend to*) and by the end of the week pretty much everybody had their own peashooter. Pea-ple were shooting peas left, right and centre. Then one afternoon during lessons, Garth Vader, one of the naughtiest boys in school, shot a pea directly at the teacher, Ms Peabody, as she reminded everyone to start thinking of ideas for the class assembly.

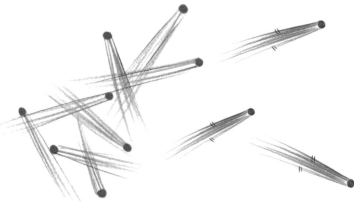

'The assembly will take the form of a debate so we'll need to come up with a topic in the next couple of days,' said Ms Peabody,

as a pea zoomed straight across the room, straight past Zareen's table and straight up Ms Peabody's left nostril! The whole class burst out laughing. Zareen felt bad for Ms Peabody, who was a really nice teacher and didn't deserve to have a pea lodged up her nose. Ms Peabody was still trying to snort the pea out when the bell rang, so Garth managed to slip out of the classroom without getting in trouble.

That break time, things went from bad to worse. Instead of just shooting peas into the air, people started shooting them directly at each other. Everyone was ducking and diving so as not to be pummelled by peas. Garth and his gang had taken to hiding behind trees so it was difficult to avoid being shot. The next day things got really out of hand . . . Instead of using squidgy fresh peas, Garth swiped a bag of frozen peas from his mum's freezer, which were much harder, much more slippery and shot out of the peashooter much faster. And they were cold too (*as frozen things tend to be*).

'Ouch!' yelled Yasmin as a stray pea hit her on the backside.

'Oh dear,' sighed Zareen. 'This is all my fault. If those pea-shooting pea-brains aren't more careful, they're gonna take somebody's eye out and –'

At that moment a single frozen pea came zooming through the air and, as if in slow motion, hit Zareen square in the eye.

Zareen burst into tears. Her eye was so sore and everything around her had gone fuzzy. Yasmin, who was always good in an emergency, took Zareen to the teacher, who took her to the nurse, who phoned Tania's work, who fetched Tania, who picked up Zareen, who said goodbye to the nurse, who sent them to the doctor, who examined her and said, 'Well, there's good news, bad news and OK news.'

'The good news is that your eye is going to be just fine. The bad news is that you're going to have to wear an eyepatch for a week or two until it heals properly. The OK news is you get a patronising sticker that says "I've seen the doctor and been a good girl".'

That night Zareen cried for ages, making her eyepatch all soggy.

'I don't want to wear an eyepatch!' she sobbed.

'We could stick some sequins on it, Princess,' suggested Tania, trying to cheer her up. 'Then everyone will be dead jealous of you at school tomorrow!'

'I don't want to go to school tomorrow,' wailed Zareen, who felt more like a pirate than a princess. 'What if someone else gets hurt by a peashooter? It'll be all my fault!'

'Well, if that's what you're worried about, crying won't help. You'll have to persuade everyone to stop using them,' said Tania.

Zareen stopped crying that very second . . . because Tania had just given her the most brilliant idea.

***

'You think the class assembly should be a debate on peashooters?' said Ms Peabody the next day.

'Yes,' replied Zareen as she explained her idea. 'I'll make the argument for why peashooters should be banned in school and someone else can make the argument for why they should be allowed. And then we'll all vote on it.'

'Well, Zareen! I think that is an excellent idea and since no one has come up with anything else, peashooters it is. Garth, seeing as you found lodging a pea into my left nostril so funny you can speak for the PPPs,' she said, chuckling.

'Huh?' said Garth, looking vacant, a look he often sported.

'The PPPs . . . the pro-peashooter people. You'll need to start your campaigns immediately and we'll hold the assembly on Friday morning.'

So Zareen put up posters with natty little slogans on them like 'No more black eyes from peas' and 'Peas hurt knees', and Garth responded by sticking up rival posters that read 'Give peas a chance' and 'Don't freeze the peas'. The school was pretty divided on the issue so when Friday came nobody had a clue who was going to win the debate.

Garth was up first, sporting his trademark vacant look and obviously feeling rather nervous.

'Errr, give peas a chance,' he said, clearing his throat.

'Yeah, we've all seen your posters,' thought Zareen, looking at Yasmin and rolling her eyes.

He then went on to make a very long-winded speech about how everyone had the right to a peashooter for self-defence, including teachers, and that all teachers should be armed with peashooters so they could shoot peas at badly behaved children.

'Peashooters can help bring discipline to this school. War and Peas!' he finished, not even making sense. Zareen noticed that this didn't go down very well with the crowd. War and peas? What on earth was he on about? Oh well, at least it helped her feel reasonably confident when it was her turn to take the stage.

'I know the risks of pea-shooting better than anyone here,' boomed Zareen, pointing at her eyepatch. 'I thought peashooters were fun at first too, but we don't need peashooters to have fun. Our ancestors didn't have peashooters and they still enjoyed break time. They played other games instead like tag and hopscotch. And to those who think they need a peashooter to defend themselves from other peashooters I say this: if someone pushes you over, is pushing them back the right thing to do? No! You tell the teacher and they sort it out. Garth talks of increased discipline, yet peashooters have brought nothing but increased chaos to this school. The statistics speak for themselves; the school nurse says playtime injuries have gone up by over a hundred per cent. We need stricter peashooter control. The current peashooter regulations are not strong enough. And so I say to you, fellow students, that we should ban peashooters from our classrooms and make our school safe again!'

There was a moment's silence in which you could have heard a pea drop – and then a spontaneous round of rapturous applause. Zareen's speech had gone down brilliantly (*as most brilliant speeches tend to*). When it came to the vote, every single person raised their hand to ban peashooters, even Garth's gang who were clearly fed up of getting covered in mushy peas.

'I'm so proud of you, Princess,' said Tania to Zareen that evening. 'I've bought you a little something to say well done for standing up and saying your peas – er, piece.'

Zareen's eyes lit up as Tania held out the '*Rapunzel*' *Fearless Fairy Tale Card* that was missing from her collection.

'You're amazing,' said Zareen, giving her step-mum an enormous hug.

That night Tania, Zareen and Dad all snuggled up together on the sofa to watch TV.

'Ouch,' yelped Zareen, pulling a small round object out from under the sofa cushion. 'Oh no, not another pea!'

'How on earth could you feel that through such a thick cushion?' asked Dad.

'Because she's a princess!' laughed Tania.

At that moment a new advert came on the TV featuring a singing and dancing Zoom Band (*basically just an overpriced elastic band*).

*'The cool kids all wear Zoom Bands*
*and you could wear some too,*
*Just beg your mums and dads to buy a pack for you!*
*Beg them good and beg them hard, that's all you have to do,*
*Then you can wear your Zoom Band and be a cool kid too!'*

'They look cool. They'll be a real hit, don't you think?' said Tania.

'Hmmm, I'm not so sure,' said Zareen, imagining a Zoom Band flying across the classroom and twanging Ms Peabody on the nose. 'I think I'll give this craze a miss.'

# Robin Hoodlum
# and his Not-So-Merry Men

Robin Hoodlum was a robbing hoodlum. He was a greedy man with a crooked little smile, a crooked little mind and a crooked little gold tooth (made entirely from snaffled gold). He would rub his hands together at even the slightest mention of money – or 'moolah' as he liked to call it. He was the kind of person who would take a teddy from a toddler or pinch the pocket money from your piggy bank when you weren't looking.

You see, Robin was a tax collector, but he only collected taxes from the poor to give to the rich – well, to his rich boss, the billionaire Baron of Bottybum. The baron was supposed to spend the money on roads, schools and hospitals for the townspeople, but he secretly spent it on bubbly beverages and beachside bungalows in the Bahamas, Bermuda and Barbados. (He loved the letter B, which is why he changed the name of his hometown of Nottingham to Bottybum.) He also loved alliteration, which, in case you don't know, is when the words in a phrase all begin with same letter – like the Pied Piper of Pamelin (*but not Hamelin because that's spelt with an H*). So anyway, as the poor got poorer and poorer, the baron and his bad buddies got richer and richer.

Because Robin was a bit of a coward, instead of collecting the taxes himself, he would send his not-so-merry men to do his dirty work for him. They were a gang of very scary and very hairy (though not very merry) men, some of whom were as tall as lamp posts but not nearly as bright. They all had a glazed look in their eyes as though they would rather be somewhere else, but as their fists were the size of footballs, nobody dared defy them.

The townspeople of Bottybum were in a terrible state. The baron had raised their taxes so high that most folk didn't have the means (money) to feed their families and had to use food banks instead (places where kind people donate food for those without it). Even the baron's own maid, Marian, had to share a single slice of stale cornbread with her daughter every night for dinner, and keep all the crumbs so there would be something left over for breakfast in the morning. But the baron didn't care and if the good folk couldn't afford to pay their taxes he would simply order Robin to take away all their possessions.

One evening, Marian was pondering the situation as she relaxed on her stone-cold floor (Robin's men had taken away her sofa). She was watching the wall (Robin's men had taken away her television). 'Where was all the money going?' she wondered. It certainly wasn't being spent on the roads as they were full of potholes. It wasn't being spent on the schools either as they'd completely run out of exercise books and desks. And it definitely wasn't being spent on hospitals because fourteen of them had closed down in the last fortnight. Marian decided to spy on the baron to see if she could get to the bottom of it.

The following day, Marian hid inside the baron's cleaning cupboard – being extra careful not to accidentally spray any Sugar and Spice and All Things Nice air freshener with her elbow or turn on the vacuum cleaner with her bottom. She waited. And waited. And waited. Marian waited all day and was about to give up when at last she heard some voices . . .

'I might go for a swim in all my lovely wonga (money),' crowed the baron. 'Those townspeople are fools if they think I'm gonna spend all this dough (money) on them when I could spend all my spondoolies (money) on me, me and, best of all . . . me! Oh, blast, botheration and bottybum, the bubbly beverages have run out. I had better raise their taxes again to bring in more dosh (money)!'

Marian couldn't believe her ears (although they'd never lied to her before) and decided to take a peek out of the cupboard door. 'Here are your wages, Robin,' said the baron, handing over a heavy bag of coins. 'And here's another bag of coins for your not-so-merry men. Keep up the terrible work!'

'Thank you, dear Baron,' said Robin, rubbing his hands

together. He emptied the contents of his
own bag into his pocket, and then,
when the baron wasn't looking,
he emptied the contents of the
second bag into his pocket as
well.

'Interesting,' thought Marian.
'He's pocketing all the money
for himself. What a rogue!'

## 'VRROOOOOM!
## VRROOOOOOOM!'

'Huh?' cried the baron.
'What's that suspicious noise?'

'Oh no!' thought Marian. 'The Hoover!' She had accidentally
turned it on with her bottom.

'Who goes there?' roared the baron.

'It's only me, your maid! I was just . . . umm . . . cleaning the
cleaning cupboard!' Marian lied, as she scuttled out of the castle.

That night, after she had tucked her daughter into the bath
(Robin's men had taken their beds away), Marian made her way to
Ye Olde Tavern. As she had suspected, Robin's not-so-merry men
were inside playing darts and drinking pints of swamp juice
(it was free, so significantly cheaper than all the other drinks).

'Hello there,' said Marian in her friendliest voice.

'Wadyawant?' slurred the most articulate of Robin's men.

'Did you get this week's wages from the baron OK?' asked Marian all innocently.

'Wadyamean? Baron dun't pay us nuffink,' replied the burly buffoon.

'Oh yes he does,' said Marian. 'The baron gives Robin a bag of money for you every week. I've seen him do it. Hmmmm . . . Unless Robin keeps it all for himself . . .'

'Wadyamean? Robin dun't pay us nuffink,' said the first one.

'Troo . . . he don't!' agreed one of the thicker men.

Robin's men looked at each other stupefied as they realised that Robin had been robbing *them*! They were so cross they all turned a funny shade of violet and steam began to pour out of their ears. It was rather unfortunate for Robin that he chose this exact moment to stroll into Ye Olde Tavern. The most hot-tempered of the men was so furious that steam was now coming out of his nostrils too. He grabbed Robin by the ankle and dangled him upside down, and, as he did so, hundreds of golden coins spilled onto the floor.

'You robbin' . . . Robin!' he yelled, pinning Robin to the dartboard.

'It was all the baron's idea!' lied Robin. 'He told me not to give you a penny.'

The men were very confused at this. They screwed up their faces and scratched their heads like they were trying to solve a particularly tricky Key Stage 6 maths problem.

'Hmmm. It's rather difficult to know who's telling the truth, Robin or the baron?' said Marian. 'Tell you what, why don't you pin them both up there? Just to be on the safe side?' she added helpfully.

'Yeh, gud idea,' grunted the men, stomping out of the tavern. Minutes later they returned, holding the Baron of Bottybum by the scruff of his cravat and pinned him up next to Robin.

'Job done!' grinned Marian. 'Now, anyone for a quick game of darts?'

When news started to spread about the fate of Robin and the baron, the townspeople jumped for joy. SINGLE MOTHER SAVES THE DAY read the headline in the *Bottybum Bugle*. Everybody's stolen money and possessions were returned to them with immediate effect (including all Marian's stolen furniture). Marian was elected as the Member of Parliament for the constituency of Bottybum with 100 per cent of the vote. She set the townspeople's taxes at a fair level and made sure it was means-tested so that the richest people paid the most. All the tax revenue was spent on roads, schools and hospitals and they all liveth happieth ever aftereth.

\*\*\*

*Epilogue:* But what of Robin's not-so-merry-men? Well, it's funny you should ask. When they were playing darts, Marian had spotted that although their fists were the size of footballs, they actually had very dainty fingers, so decided to award them a grant to open their own hairdressing salon, which had long been a secret dream of theirs. So instead of being known as the not-so-merry men they became the not-so-hairy men and the glazed look in their eyes was replaced with a sparkle. They all became very coiffured, inventing sophisticated new hairstyles such as the man-bun and the hipster moustache. People flocked for miles and miles to visit their salon, including the king, who awarded them the royal seal of approval for his high fade and stylish sideburns.

# Gretel and Hansel

Gretel and Hansel were sort of similar siblings. They both had curly caramel-coloured hair and fun-loving, freckled faces. They both wore striking stripy sweaters with trendy tight trousers. They both loved sucking sugary, sherbet-y sweets and neither of them liked their whinging, whining boss, Winnie. Oh, and most importantly, they were both born on the same superbly sunny Saturday at the start of September. That's right, Gretel and Hansel were twins. Similar, but not identical twins, because identical twins have to be either *both* boys or *both* girls.

They certainly weren't the same, just sort of similar (no two people are the same – not even identical twins). In fact, there were many differences between them. Gretel's striking stripy sweaters were often pink and purple polyester polo necks, while Hansel's were mainly monochrome and made from mohair. Gretel liked licking lusciously lemony lollipops, while Hansel favoured fantastically fizzy flying saucers. Of all their differences, Gretel's favourite was that she was one minute older and one millimetre taller than her (*quite literally*) little brother. Truth be told, she was braver and bolder too.

Gretel and Hansel worked in a sweet shop every Saturday to earn themselves a little bit of extra pocket money. Now, to most people this probably sounds like the best job ever invented in the whole of human history. Just think, you'd be surrounded by glass jars of juicy gobstoppers and tantalising tooth-tormenting treats and whenever the shop was shut you could load up with lots of lovely liquorice laces, handfuls of humbugs, clutches of candy canes and bazillions of bubblegum balls, not to mention batches of beautiful buttery butterscotch, massively minty mints, mouth-watering marzipan and marvellously mushy marshmallows.

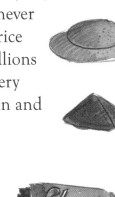

You'd think a job like this would mean sweet treats on tap . . . but I'm afraid to say there is nothing sweet about how they were treated. Gretel and Hansel's boss Winnie was a weathered, withered woman with a terse tongue and a broken brown broom that she used to jab them with whenever they weren't working hard enough. Worse still, they weren't allowed to eat ANY of the sweets. EVER. Not even the ones that were at the end of their sell-by dates. Instead, she'd feed those to her bonkers and barmy black cat, Cola Cube, who only ever ate sweets (*bonkers, I know*) his favourite being cola cubes (*barmy, I know*). To make matters worse, Winnie kept an exceptionally eager eagle eye on

100

GRETEL AND HANSEL

her CCTV monitors to make sure that the twins didn't eat any sweets at all.

What Gretel resented most, however, was that Winnie paid Hansel more handsomely than her, even though they did exactly the same job and worked exactly the same hours. How could that be fair?

So, one day, Gretel decided to confront Winnie about the matter. She had to pluck up all her courage to get the words out of her mouth.

'WhydypymlssthnHnslwhnwdthsmjb?' mumbled Gretel under her breath.

'Speak up, girl!' snapped Winnie. 'You're talking gobstopperdigook!'

22

'Why-do-you-pay-me-less-than-Hansel-when-we-do-the-same-job?' garbled Gretel at supersonic speed.

'Because,' said Winnie, rather taken aback, 'because . . . well . . . because Hansel is a strong, strapping, muscly lad who carries colossal crates of candy and confectionary up from the slippery, slimy cellar.'

'But I could do that too!' shouted Gretel, louder than she meant to.

'I don't want to hear another word on the subject,' said Winnie. 'Now, get back to work before I bosh your butt with my broken brown broomstick.'

Gretel was livid! This was even more unfair than the time that her mother blamed her for leaving a trail of breadcrumbs all over the house when it was actually Hansel who'd had a secret Sunday snacking session and had forgotten to hoover up after himself.

The following Saturday, Winnie left work early to see her cheery chiropodist, Chuck, about her

cobbled calluses and crusty corns, leaving Hansel and Gretel to lock up. It had been a long day and Gretel had just covered over the sweets with a sheet and turned the sign on the door from OPEN – COME ON IN! to GO AWAY! CAN'T YOU SEE WE'RE CLOSED? when she spotted something suspect on the CCTV. Somebody shady was skulking around in the cellar. The figure was wearing a striking stripy sweater in monochromatic material, so at first Gretel thought it might be Hansel. But it simply couldn't be because Hansel was meticulously mopping up crushed candy canes and broken banoffee brittle from the sugary sweet shop floor. On closer inspection, Gretel noticed that the figure was holding a large sack with the word SWAG printed on it in huge letters.

'Jumping jelly gems!' thought Gretel. 'It's a thief!'

Gretel darted to the shop floor to tell Hansel, who immediately fainted on the spot. Gretel rolled her eyes – she supposed she would just have to confront the thief herself. Quick-thinking Gretel grabbed the sheet covering the sweets and crept down the cellar stairs, making sure to remove her clogs, which would have made a clip-clopping clatter and given the game away. Gretel covered herself with the sweet sheet and screamed 'BOO!' at the top of her voice.

The bungling bonbon burglar looked like he'd just seen a gargantuan ghost and also fainted on the spot, falling onto the slippery, slimy floor.

'Oh great, now I have two conked-out coconut heads on my hands,' thought Gretel, as she tied the thief's hands together with some strawberry laces, hoiked him over her shoulder and carried him up the cellar stairs. 'He's heaps heavier than hauling kilos of candy,' she thought to herself.

Gretel called the police and when Winnie heard the sound of sirens she sprinted out of the chiropodist's and up the street in her bare feet to see what all the commotion was about. The police explained how Gretel had saved the day by tying up the sweetie-swiping scoundrel and hauling him up the stairs all by herself. Winnie was thrilled and instantly raised Gretel's pay, promising to treat Gretel as an equal from now on. Gretel was delighted that at last she'd be on the same pay as Hansel and she promised her mum she wouldn't spend it all on sweets.

'Oi!' wailed Winnie, jabbing Hansel with her broken brown broomstick. 'Wake up, you dizzy dingbat!'

'Winnie, could I ask for one more thing, please?' said Gretel.

'Of course, my dear,' replied Winnie in the sweetest, syrupy sugar-coated voice Gretel had ever heard her use.

'Could Hansel and I have one free sweet per day, please?'

'Well . . . seeing as you saved my superbly successful sweet shop . . . you can help yourself to free sweets whenever you like.'

Winnie winked at Gretel, who couldn't believe what she'd just heard and fainted on the spot.

# Spinocchio

Signor Spinocchio was an Italian TV news anchor. Although you might know the word 'anchor' better as the big metal hook that stops a ship moving around in the ocean, it's also the word for the main presenter of the news. When words are spelt the same or sound the same but have different meanings, they're called homonyms. Hang on, where were we . . . ? Ah yes, that's right, back to Signor Spinocchio.

Signor Spinocchio read the news out live on television at precisely six o'clock each evening. The trouble was, it had been a slow news year so there wasn't much to report, and ratings had taken a nosedive. This week's headlines were especially dull . . .

To make matters worse Signor Spinocchio was a terribly wooden presenter: unnatural and without much personality. Listening to a wooden puppet read out the recipe for spaghetti bolognaise would have been more entertaining.

Sly Fox, Signor Spinocchio's boss and president of Fox's News Network (FNN for short), was becoming increasingly impatient with Spinocchio's appalling ratings.

'Millions of viewers used to watch this show and now there are only ten! And one of them is my *nonna*!' shouted Sly.

Signor Spinocchio shrugged. 'It's not my fault. I don't make up the news!'

'That's it!' screeched Sly gleefully. 'From now on you must make up the news!'

'Isn't that just . . . lying?' said Spinocchio, who wasn't sure that this was a good idea at all.

'It's not lying!' replied Sly. 'It's simply taking the truth and twisting it. Adding a bit of spin. That's what news is all about these days. Spin, Spin-occhio, spin!'

Now, by 'spin' Sly Fox didn't mean the type of spinning that turned straw into gold, he meant influencing people. Same word, two different meanings – another homonym. But not a synonym, which is two different words with the same meaning (such as *spin* and *rotate*, or *sweater* and *jumper*). And certainly not a spinonym, which is a nonsense word we just made up.

Hang on, where were we again? Ah, that's right, back to Signor Spinocchio.

That evening, at precisely six o'clock, Signor Spinocchio read out the news live on TV and when he reached the last story, he told a little white lie.

'And finally, it has been discovered that . . . umm . . . err . . . eating chocolate and marshmallow pasta every day is very good for your health. *Ciao* for now!'

Signor Spinocchio didn't feel at all happy about *lying* to the nation and he didn't sleep very well that night. In fact, he spent most of it *lying* awake in bed. Oh, look – two different meanings of the word 'lying' spelt exactly the same way – what's that called again? (*Oh yeah . . . it's a homonym.*)

When his alarm clock went off the next morning, Signor Spinocchio rushed straight to the mirror (*as TV anchors often do*) to check he hadn't woken up with big bags under his eyes. Thankfully, there weren't any bags, but he did notice that something wasn't quite right with his nose. Was it just a little bit . . . bigger than usual? 'Who knows?' thought Signor Spinocchio. (*'Knows' not 'nose'. Two words that sound the same but are spelt differently, and mean different things – that's called a heterograph for those of you who are taking notes.*)

'Noses don't just grow overnight! It takes years for a nose to grow,' he thought to himself, applying a dash of concealer before heading off to work.

When Spinocchio eventually arrived at FNN HQ, Sly Fox was waiting for him at the door with a giant panetone (*a type of Italian cake, in case you didn't know*).

'Thank you for the cake but it's not my birthday,' said a confused Spinocchio.

'No,' said Sly, 'but it feels like mine! The ratings have rocketed! They've gone sky high! Through the roof! Everybody's talking about your chocolate and marshmallow pasta story! Every shop in the country has sold out of them and that's all anyone is eating in restaurants nationwide!'

'Oh dear,' said Spinocchio, 'but that story was a lie! Of course it's not good for you to eat chocolate and marshmallow pasta every day!'

'Eating chocolate and marshmallow pasta makes people happy, and happy people are healthy people!' said Sly. 'It's just a bit of spin! Aren't you pleased?'

'Yes,' said Spinocchio, lying, and suddenly he felt a strange sensation in his nose as if his nostrils were expanding. He shrugged it off and sloped away to the newsroom to prepare for that evening's show.

'Don't forget,' Sly called after him. 'Take the truth and twist it. Twist it right round like fusilli.' (*Fusilli is a type of twisted Italian pasta, in case you were wondering.*)

That evening on the six o'clock bulletin, Spinocchio lied once again.

'And finally,' said Spinocchio, broadcasting live to everyone in Italy, 'it has been revealed that . . . umm . . . err . . . the prime minister is an alien. *Ciao* for now!'

Extra clever readers might have spotted that although they are spelt the same, the first 'L-I-V-E' in the previous sentence is pronounced *lyve* and the second 'L-I-V-E' is pronounced *liv*. That makes it a heteronym, which means two words that are spelt the same but are pronounced differently and have different meanings. Like live (*lyve*) and live (*liv*) or windy (*windi*) and windy (*wyndi*). Now where were we? Oh yes . . .

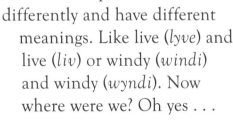

'Ouch!' cried Spinocchio as the show came off air. 'I think my nose is swelling up.'

113

And at that very moment Spinocchio's nose swelled to double its usual size.

'What in Geppetto's half-moon spectacles is happening to *il mio bel naso?*' cried Spinocchio. 'I shouldn't be able to see my own nose without looking in a mirror!'

'Oh dear,' said Sly. 'It does appear to have grown longer than a grissini.' (*That's a type of Italian breadstick.*) 'Oh well. Not to worry. The ratings are in and I can officially announce we are the most watched show in the whole of Italy! Can you believe it?'

'Really?' said Spinocchio, momentarily distracted. 'Are we really the most watched show on Italian TV?'

'Yes, my boy,' cried Sly. 'You are now the most famous news anchor in all of Italy. Here's a Ferrari to celebrate!'

Spinocchio was confused. He didn't like lying, but he did like being the most famous news anchor in all of Italy. But then again, he didn't like his sneaking suspicion that every time he lied his nose grew bigger . . . But then again, he did like being the most famous news anchor in Italy A LOT! What a dilemma!

The next morning Spinocchio sat at his kitchen table with a cappuccino (*a type of Italian coffee*) and some biscotti (*a type of Italian biscuit*) to read the front page of the daily newspaper:

# ALIEN
## PRIME MINISTER
# ARRESTED!

It was revealed last night on FNN that our very own prime minister is, in fact, an alien. Since we cannot have an alien in charge of Italy, the authorities have put him in jail and thrown the key into Lake Como (the deepest lake in Italy) just to be on the safe side.

'Oh dear,' thought Spinocchio. 'The poor prime minister!' He wasn't an alien in either sense of the word. You see, 'alien' can either mean you belong to a different country or you are literally from another planet. (*It's a homonym – same word, two different meanings, remember?*) The poor prime minister was neither of these things and he was now languishing in a dingy prison cell. 'This is the last straw,' thought Spinocchio.

'Enough is enough,' Spinocchio said to Sly Fox after speeding to work in his new Ferrari. 'I refuse to make up nonsense news ever again. Not only is my nose now the length of linguini (*another type of Italian pasta*) but the poor prime minister is being punished for no good reason! And you don't seem to give a flying focaccia!' (*A focaccia is a type of Italian bread, in case you were about to ask.*)

'My dear boy,' said Sly in an oily voice that Spinocchio did not like very much. 'If you do not lie on my news bulletin tonight, then I'm afraid you will be in very serious trouble.'

'I don't care!' shouted Spinocchio. 'I will never tell another lie again as long as I live.'

## BONK!

His nose hit the computer screen in front of him.

'Do you know the two meanings of the word "fire"?' said Sly in a sinister tone. 'Well, if you don't lie on this evening's show, then I'm afraid I will have to fire you. Then set fire to your Ferrari. You don't mind lying after all, do you, Spinocchio?' he asked menacingly.

'No,' lied Spinocchio as his nose shot out the other side of the computer screen and hit the wall.

Spinocchio was at a loss. It seemed like he didn't have any choice but to lie. He simply couldn't afford to lose his job nor could he bear to lose his beloved Ferrari. When six o'clock came round he told the truth the entire way through the news bulletin but just as he was approaching the last story, he noticed Sly Fox holding up a sign behind the camera: LIE OR I'M SETTING YOUR FERRARI ON FIRE! (MWAH-HA-HA!)

'And finally,' said Spinocchio, staring down the barrel of the lens, 'it has been revealed that . . . umm . . . err . . . the sky is falling in. *Ciao* for now.'

And at that very moment Spinocchio's nose went shooting through the lens of the camera!

'Woohoo!' cried Sly Fox. 'The ratings are in and we're now the most watched show in the entire world! Global domination is finally mine! He punched his fist in the air in a maniacal fashion.

Spinocchio felt dreadful about lying to the entire world that the sky was falling in. Worse still, his nose had now grown so long that people kept trampling over it. Everyone was running around like headless chicken-lickens, panicking about the sky's imminent implosion. Some people hid under their beds, some dug up their kitchen floors to build underground shelters, while others panic-bought lifetime supplies of food and toilet roll in case they could never go outside ever again. It was complete and utter chaos.

Spinocchio knew he had to do something and luckily at precisely six o'clock he would have complete control of the airwaves!

That evening, in his usual slot, Spinocchio broadcast a special news bulletin.

'*Signore e signori*, ladies and gentlemen,' said Spinocchio, addressing the entire population of the world, 'I have an apology to make. I'm afraid the news hasn't been quite up to scratch lately. In fact, you could say it's been fake news. Eating chocolate and marshmallow pasta every day isn't good for you, the prime minister is not an alien, and the sky is definitely not falling in. I'm very sorry for lying but Sly Fox threatened to fire me and set fire to my beautiful Ferrari.'

And, as if by magic, Spinocchio's nose shrank back to its original size.

'**Noooooooooooooooo!**' screamed Sly Fox as the *carabinieri* (*that's the Italian police*) carted him off to prison. They also sent a team of deep-sea divers to the bottom of Lake Como to retrieve the key to the prime minister's cell and set him free.

Spinocchio breathed a huge sigh of relief. Lying was exhausting! Telling the truth felt so much better.

The next morning when the daily newspapers landed on the nation's doorsteps, everyone was greeted by truthful headlines that for once weren't boring.

# FAKE NEWS NETWORK FLOPS!
## A WIN-OCCHIO FOR SPINOCCHIO!
### FROM FNN TO *KGT*

Signor Spinocchio quits FNN, or what he calls the 'Fake News Network', to become the new presenter of Italy's very own version of *Kingdom's Got Talent*.

Signor Spinocchio commented: 'People need to be very careful not to believe everything they hear on the news or read in the papers. Not all of it is true and sometimes people have reasons for lying, so always check your facts! I can't wait to start my new job. I love all the different acts, especially the dancing ones because if there's one thing that definitely is true it's that hips don't lie.'

# Snow White and the Five-a-Side Football Team

Snow White was a serious footie fan. She ate, slept and breathed football. (*Well, she didn't actually eat, sleep or breathe footballs – that would be weird – it's what we call a metaphor, and it just means that she really loved football.*) When it came to football, the only thing Snow White didn't do was play it. It wasn't that she didn't want to play the beautiful game – it was just that where she lived, only boys played football, and she wasn't sure if she would match up. Sometimes, when everyone else was asleep, she would secretly practise in her backyard, but she would never dream of doing keepy-uppies or a scissor kick in daylight in case people laughed at her.

Snow White lived with five lads – Sporty, Ginger, Baby, Scary and Posh – who all played on a five-a-side football team together. Although she didn't play on the team herself, Snow White would always go along to their matches to cheer them on and celebrate with them when they won. Unfortunately, they never won. Yep, that's right! The team had lost every single match they'd ever played. That's 17,836 games in total. They were currently languishing at the bottom of the league table and if they didn't win their next match against their arch rivals, the Poisoned Apples, they'd be kicked out of the league altogether.

Worried about the team's misfortune, Snow White knew that she was their only hope. She had to figure out exactly why they kept losing and put the puff back into their very deflated football.

So, after kick-off one afternoon, instead of cheering the lads on, Snow White made notes about their individual performances on the pitch.

**SPORTY** - Sport comes to him naturally. Boundless energy and stamina. Good in any position.

**GINGER** - Approaches the game gingerly but nonetheless lives up to his nickname the 'ginger ninja'. Stealth moves, great in goal.

**BABY** - Tiny but perfectly formed. Spectacular at dribbling. A perfect midfielder.

**SCARY** - Petrifying moves. The other team are terrified of his talent. Frighteningly good striker.

**POSH** – So polite he often passes the ball to the opposing team. More concerned about getting his strip muddy than scoring. Has unknowingly scored nineteen own goals while apologising to others for getting in their way. Shockingly bad in every position.

'Aha!' thought Snow White, looking back over her notes. 'I've hit the nail on the head!' (*She hadn't actually hit a nail on the head – it's another metaphor, meaning that she'd realised what the problem was. And in this case the problem was Posh.*)

At half-time, she huddled together with the lads in the changing rooms to share her findings before the crucial second half. Although they were losing nineteen–nil, Snow White had a cunning plan . . .

'All we need to do is make a substitution,' she said.

'But we don't have any substitutes,' replied Sporty. 'There are only five of us.'

'Six, actually,' said Snow White. 'If you count me. I'll play in the second half and Posh can sit on the bench.'

The five lads burst out laughing. They laughed so loudly it reminded Snow White of the evil queen's wicked cackle. Snow White wanted the ground to swallow her up. (*That's a metaphor too, by the way – she didn't actually want the ground to swallow her up; she just didn't want to be there because she felt so embarrassed.*)

'Football's for boys!' cried Baby.

'Yeah,' chimed in Sporty. 'Girls can't play football.'

Snow White was furious. Why couldn't girls play football? Girls had legs, didn't they? And brains? She took a deep breath, then using her very sizeable brain worked out exactly what she needed to do . . .

'Do you like watching TV, Sporty?' asked Snow White.

'I LOVE TV!' replied Sporty. 'Especially *Kingdom's Got Talent!*'

'Hmm,' said Snow White. 'Well, that's not very sporty, is it? How about you, Scary, do you like hugging people?'

'Hugging's my favourite!' replied Scary.

'Hmmm,' said Snow White. Well, that's not very scary, is it?'

'I don't understand,' cried Baby. 'Why is this relevant?'

'You can't always judge a book by its cover,' explained Snow White. (*She wasn't saying the lads were books. It was yet another metaphor. She meant you can't always judge things by their labels.*)

'Just because your name is Baby it doesn't mean you wear nappies and cry all the time. And just because Ginger is called Ginger doesn't mean that his favourite spice is ginger.'

'No!' cried Ginger. 'My favourite spice is star anise. I like garam masala too – but technically that's a blend of spices.'

'And just because I'm a girl doesn't mean I can't play football,' said Snow White.

The lads looked at each other and the penny dropped. (*Not an actual penny – it's another metaphor. Basically, it means they understood what Snow White meant.*)

'You should definitely play in the second half, Snow White,' said Posh. 'To be perfectly honest, I don't really like playing football that much.'

'Yes!' agreed the others. 'Snow White should play. But hurry up, the second half has already started and we're still in the changing room!'

Snow White whipped off her outfit like there was no tomorrow (*there was a tomorrow; it's just another metaphor, which means she did it quickly*) to reveal that she was wearing her football kit underneath – she always wore it just in case! She sprinted onto the pitch where she was like a fish in water (*that's another*

*metaphor – she obviously wasn't a fish, let alone one in water – it just means that she was a natural footballer*). She ran rings around the Poisoned Apples, and even their star player, Golden Balls Delicious, couldn't stop her from scoring GOAL after GOAL after GOAL after GOAL after GOAL after GOAL after GOAL after GOAL after GOAL after GOAL after GOAL after GOAL after GOAL after GOAL after GOAL after GOAL after GOAL after GOAL after GOAL after GOAL after GOAL after GOAL.

When the final whistle blew, Snow White and the team won the match twenty-nineteen and Snow White was awarded 'Man of the Match'. (*That wasn't a metaphor; they actually did mean 'man' so the league officials decided to change it to 'Person of the Match' for all future games.*)

Posh was very relieved he never had to play football ever again. In fact, he ended up marrying Golden Balls Delicious who, despite being in the rival team, wasn't a bad apple at all. He was a good egg. (*He wasn't actually an egg or an apple – yep, you guessed it, they're just metaphors meaning he was 'a good person'.*) And it goes to show you can't judge a book by its cover. Although you can with this book as it has an excellent cover.

# THE THREE LITTLE PUGS

If you take a turn down Leprechaun Lane,
Then go past the toy shop, and turn right again,
You'll come to a place that's a bit of a dive,
A street that is known as Doggyturn Drive.

It's littered with bones and covered in hair,
With chew toys and fur on the ground everywhere,
And living at property 1-0-1D,
Are three doggy housemates who we're off to see.

So please say hello to the three little pugs,
With squashed little snouts on their squished little mugs.
The blonde one's called Straw, the red one is Brick,
And Woody's the one who looks a bit thick.

Last week someone knocked on the door of their place,
And they opened it wide to a big scary face:
The big, bad wolf who had leased them their flat
Was stood in his long pug-fur coat with fur hat.

'I'm afraid that I have to increase all the rent
By a total amount of nine hundred per cent.'
'We don't have the money!' cried out Straw and Brick.
('Wot's rent?' Woody asked, as he chewed on a stick.)

Poor Brick and poor Straw started freaking right out
(While Woody was trying to lick his own snout).
'He's being so greedy – he's being so mean.
He owns far more land than the king and the queen.'

Where would they live? They couldn't pay more . . .
Beneath a wood pile? Or under some straw?
'I've got it!' cried Woody, as quick as a flash.
'Let's climb in this dustbin and live in the trash!'

'We need something sturdy and made out of brick.
Just use your brain, Woody, and stop being thick!'
'Why don't the three of us all just stay here?
I don't wanna leave and the rent isn't dear.'

The other two pugs were now close to despair.
'We need an idea, oh this just isn't fair.'
'I have it!' cried Brick, like his team had just scored.
'Let's contact the Canine Advisory Board!'

The board met the pugs and examined their lease.
The small print explained that they couldn't be fleeced.
If your rent's to go up, then you need three years' warning.
Brick and Straw cheered (while Woody was yawning).

The next day the wolf came, all suited and booted
(He'd bought brand-new clothes with the money he'd looted).
They showed him their contract, then showed him the door,
   Then changed all the locks, you know, just to be sure.

   Wolf huffed and he puffed and he puffed and he huffed,
   But the law is the law and the pugs were just chuffed,
   Cos greed doesn't pay and villains will fail,
   So don't be like the wolf or you'll end up in jail.

   And that is the tale of the three little pugs,
   Who ended their day with some high fives and hugs.
   'All right then,' said Woody, 'thank goodness for that.
   Now when do we have to move out of our flat?'

# The Pickled Mermaid

Arielle was in a bit of a pickle. She was the very last free-swimming mermaid in the entire ocean. All the others had been trapped in oil slicks and human pollution. Since people had stopped treating the ocean with respect and started throwing plastic bags and bottles into it willy-nilly, the sea was no longer a fun place to be. Arielle's greatest fear was that she would end up as an exhibit in a museum, pickled in a giant jar labelled:

*Arielle Anchovy*
*The Last Ever Mermaid*

Arielle was mute, which meant she couldn't speak. Whenever she tried to talk, bubbles appeared from her mouth instead of words – and not even speech bubbles, just air bubbles. Arielle didn't suppose it mattered much, since there weren't any other mermaids or mermen to speak to any more. She did have other fishy friends, of course; her favourite being Shakira the Surprisingly Sociable Shark who she spoke to using sign language. She and Shakira would ponder the perils of global warming and debate the dangers of plastic pollution for hours on end. Arielle loved that they could have private conversations and share secrets that others wouldn't understand – there weren't that many signers in the ocean as it's a lot trickier with fins as opposed to fin-gers. (*Most octopuses are pretty good at it, though.*)

One day, as Arielle was doing the washing up (*which is pretty easy when you live in the ocean*), a horrible darkness descended on the surface of the sea. At first Arielle thought the sun had decided to go to bed early but when she looked closer she realised that black gloopy oil was spilling from a hole in the bottom of a massive tanker. The oil was spreading at a great speed, as if someone had poured a giant pot of black paint into the sea, and hundreds of fish were getting stuck in the sticky black liquid.

Suddenly, Arielle spotted Shakira swimming straight towards the oil, totally oblivious - she hadn't noticed it!

'Shakira! Watch out! Don't swim into the oil spill!' Arielle would have screamed if she could have. But, alas, she couldn't scream and all that came out of her mouth were a few silent bubbles. So, Shakira the Surprisingly Sociable Shark just kept on swimming straight into the oil, where she met a very sticky end. 'Poor Shakira,' thought Arielle, tears flowing down her cheeks. 'Of all the sharks in all the world to have lost, why her?' Sometimes life was so unfair.

A darkness spread in Arielle's mind just like the black oil that had spread across the sea. She felt so sad about her poor friend Shakira and so angry that humans were destroying their own planet with oil spills and plastic bottles. And this was just the tip of the iceberg (*talking of icebergs, because of climate change they were all melting!*). Arielle knew that human actions and behaviour were destroying the earth's atmosphere and warming up the planet. Species were dying out, sea levels were rising and pollution was making air unhealthy to breathe. If someone didn't act soon those changes would become irreversible. She had to do something about it. But what? How could she tell them to stop destroying the ocean when she couldn't even speak a single word out loud? The world's biggest megaphone made out of a giant shell wouldn't get her heard.

An anxious Arielle decided to check her Plaicebook to make sure her other friends were OK. That was when the answer struck her. She would use seashell media to get her message out there. Plaicebook, Finstagram, Snapperchat – she had accounts with all of them. She immediately recorded a vlog with her shellfie stick all about what was happening in the ocean and added subtitles for those who couldn't understand sign language. She explained how barracuda were mistaking bits of plastic for plants, how octopuses were getting their tentacles trapped in carrier bags, how non-biodegradable rubbish was getting caught on coral and how her poor friend Shakira had swum into a terrible oil spill.

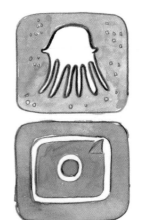

Arielle posted the video on YouTuna and before long it went viral and people started cleaning up their act. No more plastic bags and bottles were thrown into the ocean. In fact, everyone stopped using single-use plastic altogether, swapping instead to biodegradable materials. Not only was the vlog seen by billions, it was played on news channels around the world (including FNN in Italy).

The Disasters and Emergencies Committee responded by setting up an appeal fund. Millions were raised to send a multinational team to clear up the oil spill and stop any more harm coming to the environment.

Eventually, after all the oil and plastic had been removed from the ocean, the mermaids, mermen and other creatures who had been trapped became free and were no longer considered endangered species. Arielle was reunited with all her old friends and family. Once more the ocean was a happy place to be and all because of Arielle's lone voice . . . well, vlog.

# THE GINGERBREAD KID

Gregory was a real joker. Everybody loved his jokes – from butchers and bakers to candlestick makers. He had a permanent grin on his face as though it had been piped on with icing sugar (*probably because it actually had been*) and big brown eyes, which were warm and welcoming just like huge velvety chocolate buttons (*probably because they actually were*). Gregory was your regular all-round funny guy except for one tiny detail . . . He was made entirely out of gingerbread. Well, except for his icing-sugar smile and chocolate-button eyes . . . oh, and his chocolate-button . . . er . . . buttons. You see, Gregory was a Gingerbread Kid.

Gregory lived in Fairy Tale Land with his parents, the Gingerbread Woman and the Gingerbread Man (*you may have heard of him, as he had a book written about him once*). Although Fairy Tale Land sounds like an idyllic place where everyone gets free kittens and lives happily ever after, the reality was far from it. Nobody seemed to get along. The big bad wolves didn't like the pigs and kept blowing their houses down. The trolls didn't like the goats and kept pushing them off bridges. And the foxes didn't like the gingerbread people and kept trying to eat them.

As if that wasn't bad enough, Gregory's family heard on the beanstalk (*like the way you or I hear gossip on the grapevine*) that his favourite uncle had been swallowed whole by a fox!

'Poor Uncle Graeme!' cried the Gingerbread Woman.

'We can't stay here a moment longer,' declared the Gingerbread Man.

So the family packed their bags and left their home to seek refuge in a new country across the sea. The boat journey was long and treacherous. They were almost capsized by a massive wave and had to avoid an enormous kraken as well as two and a half pirate ships.

Gregory tried to lighten the mood by telling a joke. 'What did the pirate say when he got his wooden leg stuck in the freezer? Shiver me timbers!'

Gregory chuckled to himself, but his parents were so worried that he might fall out of the boat and go all soggy that they couldn't even muster the tiniest titter. However, luck was on their side, and after days and days and days and days and days and days at sea, they finally made it to dry land and a small town called Bakewell.

Although Gregory was sad that he would never see Fairy Tale Land again, he was looking forward to making lots of friends at his new school. He was so excited, in fact, that on the first day of term Gregory (a keen amateur baker) woke up an extra three hours early to bake his classmates chocolate doughnuts. 'I hope the kids there like me!' he thought. 'And if they don't, they're just a bunch of doughnuts.' He giggled and licked some chocolate off his wooden spoon.

'Break a leg, my little cookie,' said the Gingerbread Man at the school gates. 'On second thoughts, don't do that. We're running low on icing sugar to stick you back together.' The Gingerbread Man kissed

Gregory goodbye and headed inside to start his new job as a dinner man at Gregory's new school.

'I suppose I had better make some new friends,' thought Gregory, as he looked around the playground and spotted a small gang of chuckling children.

'They look like a laugh,' he thought, skipping over to them and offering them each a doughnut from his box, though not before throwing in a joke to break the ice!

'What does bread do when it's bored?' he asked. 'Loaf around! Get it? Loaf? Bread?' But instead of laughing, as people usually did at Gregory's jokes, the children started shrieking.

'Eugh! We don't want doughnuts that have been touched by a gingerbread kid! They'll taste all horrible and gingery!'

'Are these kids bananas?' wondered Gregory. 'Ginger tastes great with chocolate.'

They clearly weren't up to date with his favourite TV show, the *Great British Cake Off*. He was about to ask them if they watched it when they all started singing.

*'Run, run, we don't care if you skid – you can't share with us, little gingerbread kid!'*

Just then, the school bell rang and the group scampered off.

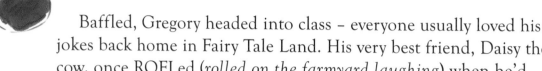

Baffled, Gregory headed into class – everyone usually loved his jokes back home in Fairy Tale Land. His very best friend, Daisy the cow, once ROFLed (*rolled on the farmyard laughing*) when he'd told her this one . . .

'What did one slice of bread say to the other when he saw the grill was on? Uh-oh, we're toast!'

Gregory entered the classroom and made his way towards the back to find an empty seat, but the kids who had been mean to him were already sitting there.

'Perhaps they misheard me,' thought Gregory. 'I'll give them a second shot.'

'Hey, you lot . . . What did the butter say to the bread? I'm on a roll! Get it? Roll? Bread?'

But the children just stared at him stony-eyed. 'Tough crowd,' thought Gregory.

'We don't want to sit with a crumby gingerbread kid,' cried the children. Then the leader of the group really took the biscuit and stood in front of Gregory's chair so Gregory couldn't sit down. 'Go away!' he spat. 'You're not like us. You're different. We don't like people who are different.'

*'Run, run, we don't care if you skid –*
*you can't sit with us, little gingerbread kid!'*

At lunchtime Gregory pushed his food around his plate gingerly. 'But pizza is your favourite! said the Gingerbread Man from behind the counter. 'Everyone else is wolfing theirs down.' But Gregory just sighed.

On his way home that day Gregory's grin had melted away.

'Hello, Gregory,' said the candlestick maker. 'Got any good jokes for me? I rather need cheering up. The candlestick business has been terrible since the advent of electricity. I'm about to go bankrupt!'

'Why don't you ask the butcher or the baker?' said Gregory as he sloped off down the street.

That night he wasn't even in the mood to watch the semi-final of the *Great British Cake Off*. One thing kept spinning round and round his mind like a whisk in a mixing bowl: why were those kids so cruel to him?

'Gregory, sweetie-pie, would you like a slice of pizza?' the Gingerbread Man called from the kitchen. 'You didn't eat any at lunchtime.'

Gregory was about to say 'No, thank you', when he was struck by the most ingenious idea.

'Dad,' asked Gregory, 'could we have pizza again for lunch at school tomorrow, please?'

'Of course, my biscuity boy. What a good idea, your favourite! That'll help cheer you up. I hate it when you feel crumby.'

And, just like that, Gregory's grin returned.

'Cheers, Dad,' he said. 'Hey, have you heard the one about the naughty baker? He got arrested for whipping the cream!'

His parents laughed so hard their heads nearly broke off.

The next morning at playtime Gregory was keen to test out a new joke he'd just invented. He looked around the playground for someone to try it out on, but before he had the chance he stumbled upon the same mean group of kids from before.

'No, not again!' he thought. 'Oh well, let's see if this one makes them laugh.'

'Why was the butter in a foul mood? He woke up on the wrong side of the bread. Get it? Bread? Bed? No? Nothing? Seriously?'

'Eugh!' shouted the horrible children. 'We don't want to hang out with a gingerbread kid! We'll get crumbs all over us!'

*'Run, run, we don't care if you skid – you can't hang with us, little gingerbread kid!'*

But Gregory wasn't bothered this time, because he had a plan that would kick into action the moment the school lunchbell ra—

# *BRRRRRRRRRIIIIIINNNNNGGGGG!*

'Woohoo! Pizza for lunch two days in a row!' exclaimed the entire school, as they queued up in the dining hall. 'I wonder what'll be on the menu tomorrow?'

Tomorrow came and nobody could believe their luck – pizza for a third day. 'It's a miracle!' they all cried. On the fourth day, though, everyone was a bit less excited. Pizza again? Really? And by the fifth day everyone was completely sick of pizza. They didn't want to see another pizza again if they lived till they were a million and one.

'Tell your dad we don't want any more pizza. We want something different!' shouted the horrible children. Gregory grinned – his ingenious plan was working . . . ingeniously!

'OK, I'll tell him,' Gregory replied. 'But I thought you didn't like things to be different? I thought you wanted everything and everyone to be exactly the same?' The children looked at each other, a bit surprised, so Gregory continued. 'Imagine if you had to have pizza for lunch every day for a year! Or if your socks were all the same, so there was only ever one colour to wear! Or what if your friends all looked and acted exactly the same? How boring would that be?'

The children understood exactly what Gregory meant and stopped being horrible that very second. When they started talking to him properly, they quickly realised that Gregory was actually the most fabulous, fascinating and funny boy in Bakewell. Suddenly, everyone wanted to be his friend; they were literally queuing up to have selfies with him as if he were a famous popstar like Rapunzel. They all had loads of questions to ask him, like did he ever nibble his own arm if he got peckish? And was it scary crossing such a big ocean in a tiny boat when they fled from Fairy Tale Land? And did Trumplestiltskin really fart off into space never to be seen again? Soon Gregory had everyone enthralled with tales from back home, of newsreaders with long noses, pugs who read their contracts and beanstalks with giants at the top.

'Speaking of giants,' said Gregory, 'what did the giant say when he sat on the biscuit? Oh, crumbs! Get it? Crumbs!'

The whole playground was FLOLing (finally laughing out loud). Gregory had become the most popular boy in school, which was the icing on the cake. By the end of the day his sugar-sweet smile was bigger than ever and his chocolate-button eyes were practically melting with happiness. (*Don't worry – they weren't* actually *melting, it's just a metaphor that means he was really happy*.)

On his way home Gregory bumped into the candlestick maker again. 'Sorry about your business going bankrupt,' said Gregory.

'No worries,' said the (now former) candlestick maker. 'Candlesticks are so yesterday. Fax machines are the future. That's the new business I'm going into. I'm in such a good mood. Go on, tell me a joke!'

'Yeah, go on,' said the baker, popping out of his shop.

'What does a baker like to drink?' said Gregory. 'Baking soda!'

'LMAO (laughing my apron off)!' said the butcher, coming out of her shop after hearing all the laughter. 'Did you make that one up?'

'Yep!' said Gregory.

'You are one smart cookie,' said the butcher. 'Here, take these beef burgers home to your parents.'

'No, thanks. My friend Daisy the cow would never speak to me again,' Gregory replied, heading off home to watch the final of the *Great British Cake Off*.

As soon as Gregory got in, he bounded into the kitchen to tell his mum and dad about his amazing day. But before he could say anything, the Gingerbread Man cried out, 'Surprise! Guess what, Gregory? I've made you your favourite dinner . . .'

'Oh no,' thought Gregory, as his dad handed him the most enormous pizza.

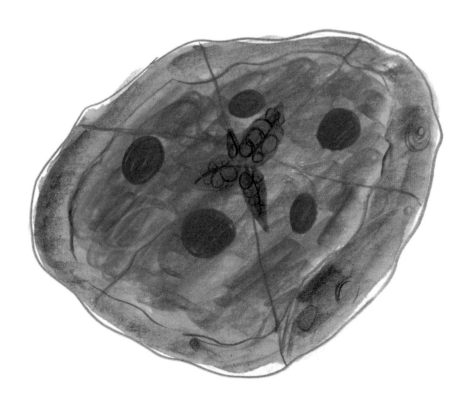

# CINDERELLA AND THE
# COMFY OLD TRAINER

Cinderella was a very determined young woman with a mind of her own. Whenever there was anything she didn't like about the world, she would try to change it. Her mother had taught her that if something isn't fair, she should try to make it fair, and that small changes can lead to big changes. So, when it was frosty, Cinderella would hand out free woollen winter wear to woodland creatures – she couldn't bear the thought of shivering squirrels clutching onto their frozen nuts while she was wrapped up all cosy and warm inside.

She once went on homework strike till her teacher changed their school topic from 'Magical Men from Many Moons Ago' to 'Prodigious People from the Past' so the class could learn about wonderful women as well as marvellous men. She had even helped raise millions of pounds in funds for an ocean clean-up campaign that saved mermaids from extinction. Cinderella believed in fairness for all, something else her beloved mother (a very wonderful woman) had taught her as a little girl.

Pay: The Merpeople

£10,000,000

Cinderella had extremely fond memories of her mother, a formidable force who had tried to help women gain the same rights as men (*which certainly wasn't the case back in the olden days and often still isn't now*). Her mother believed that women should be able to vote in elections and go out to work and do whatever they wanted, back when lots of men thought they should only be allowed to do cooking and cleaning. Boring!

'Never forget the suffragettes – they fought to give us women our rights,' her mother had always said. And although her mother wasn't around any more, Cinderella still remembered her motto: Deeds Not Words.

After Cinderella's mum died, her dad got a new girlfriend who already had two daughters, Kim and Chloe. Kim and Chloe thought that Cinderella should have to do all the cooking and cleaning as they were far too busy putting on make-up, buying clothes and filming their new reality TV show (all about them putting on make-up and buying clothes).

So, it should come as no surprise at all that they were both **'Oh my gawsh! Totally, awesomely amazed'** to find out that the king was holding a 'princess party' to choose the ideal girl for the prince to marry, and all three sisters were invited.

'Oooooh,' they cooed. 'We'd better buy yet more make-up and yet more clothes! And, Cinders, you'll have to stop wearing those yucky old trainers. Maybe we could give you a makeover! Oh, Cinders, can we please?'

'No, thanks,' replied Cinderella curtly.

Kim and Chloe gawped in disbelief. Who in their right mind wouldn't want a makeover from them?

'What kind of prince holds a knees-up just so he can handpick his "perfect" woman? Prince Charmless, that's who!' declared Cinderella, throwing the flyer straight into the fire. 'There's absolutely no way I'm going to this so-called ball. I'd rather stay at home and do my chores – and that's saying something!'

But Kim and Chloe had already stopped listening and had rushed upstairs for some urgent pampering. Cinderella, on the other hand, donned her bright yellow Marigolds and set to work cleaning the bathroom around them.

Later on, as her sisters got ready for the party, trying on yet more clothes and plastering on yet more make-up, Cinderella headed back downstairs to make a start on the stove. As she scrubbed at some ovengrit that was almost as stubborn as Cinderella herself, the room started to fill with a haze of purple, white and green smoke. For a moment Cinderella thought perhaps there had been a dangerous chemical reaction involving her mild green Beary Liquid, but then she heard a voice from behind her.

'What on earth are you doing here, young lady?'

'Mum? Is that you?' exclaimed Cinderella, turning round. 'What on earth are *you* doing here on Earth?'

'I've been sent back as your fairy good-mother, to make sure you do good. I always raised you to do the right thing in life and I'm not about to stop now.'

'I'm not going to that ridiculous ball, if that's what you mean,' replied Cinderella.

'Oh yes you are!' said her mum.

'Oh no I'm not!' said Cinderella.

'Oh yes you are,' said her mum. 'And what do you think this is? A pantomime? You shall go to the ball . . . to protest against it! I brought you up to stand up for what you believe in, so get those rubber gloves off your mitts and get out there!' And with one whoosh of her magic wand, she magicked Cinderella's wheelchair into a snazzy van with loudspeakers on top and huge lettering on the side that read REAL PRINCES DON'T THROW PRINCESS PARTIES. And with a second whoosh of her wand, she turned the rubber gloves into hot pumpkin sandwiches in case the protest went on into the small hours. 'Now get going,' said Cinderella's mum, 'or you'll be late for your own protest!'

When Cinderella
finally arrived at the
palace, the first thing she
spotted was a huge banner
hung above the gates.
It read: THE OFFICIAL ROYAL
PRINCESS PARTY! WHO WILL
MARRY THE PRINCE? IT COULD
BE YOU! Cinderella drove
straight over, whipped off
one of her trainers and flung
it at the banner, knocking it down.

'Whoooaaaaa! Watch where you're throwing your footwear!'
someone shouted, ducking out of the way of the trainer as it landed
with a *splosh* in the palace moat.

'Oops! Sorry!' said Cinderella, looking up. 'Hang about, don't
I know you from somewhere? Didn't you get to judges' houses on
season seventeen of *Kingdom's Got Talent?*'

'No, I'm the prince! That's why you recognise me.'

'Oh no you're not!' replied Cinderella.

'Oh yes I am!' replied the prince.

'Look, this isn't a pantomime!' said Cinderella, 'and if you are
the prince, then you should know that REAL princes DON'T
throw princess parties.'

Cinderella was just about to give the prince a piece of her mind and start lecturing him about modern-day women, when she spotted something strange . . . The prince was holding a pole in his left hand . . . and at the top of the pole was a sign that read: REAL PRINCES DON'T THROW PRINCESS PARTIES, and in his right hand he was clutching another that read: PRINCESS PARTIES ARE PANTS! Cinderella grinned as she realised what was going on: the prince was protesting against his own party!

The prince explained that the party was all his dad's idea; he and his mum thought it was completely old-fashioned and outdated. To make matters more outrageous, the prince told Cinders that he didn't actually want to marry to a princess and would much rather marry a handsome prince instead! Cinderella and the prince found that they got on like a palace on fire and chatted away about

anything and everything, from her mum to the Suffragettes to palace life, right through to her collection of old trainers. The prince even commented that he'd noticed she had cool trainers (*well, trainer, now that one was floating in the moat*).

'Hmmmm . . .' said the prince after a while. 'This protest doesn't seem to be working.'

'Deeds not words!' said Cinders. 'Let's step things up a notch.' The prince and Cinders set about chaining the van to the palace gates and began chanting: 'Real princes don't have princess parties!' They honked the horn furiously and soon the king and all the ballgoers poured out onto the palace steps.

'What in the name of Trumplestiltskin is going on?' boomed the king, who then turned to Cinderella and said, 'And where's your other trainer?'

'I told you I didn't want a princess party!' cried the prince.

'It's old-fashioned and outdated,' chipped in Cinders.

'I told you so,' gloated the queen, who then turned to Cinderella and said: 'And where is your other trainer?'

'But these girls all want to marry our son,' protested the king.

'Nah, we just love a good party!' giggled Chloe, who then added, 'and, by the way, hun, that one-trainer look is not a good one, Cindy.'

'Yeah, OMG, we LOVE a #goodparty, LOL,' agreed Kim. 'Especially one that's totally amazingly awesome footage for our reality show and our soon-to-be-launched UsTube channel!'

'Oh . . .' said the king. 'Does *anyone* here want to marry our son or are you just here for the free food, banging tunes and a snoop around the royal palace?'

All the partygoers coughed and looked around nervously.

'Hmm. I think I may have misjudged this one,' conceded the king. 'But let's not allow the hot buffet to go to waste, eh? Why don't we forget about the princess bit and carry on where we left off?'

'Hear, hear!' added the queen. 'As of today, there will be no more princess parties! Now let's party like it's 1918, the year some women were first granted the right to vote!'

Everyone cheered and piled back into the palace.

'Hey, Cinds,' said Kim. 'Just out of, you know, interest, where is that missing trainer?'

'It's behind you,' replied Cinderella.

'Where?' said Kim, turning round and surveying the area. 'Oh no it's not!'

'Oh yes it is,' answered Cinders. 'It's in the moat. Long story . . .'

'Best place for it!' said Chloe, giggling. 'You should stick the other one in there too.'

Cinderella and the prince celebrated their victory with a good gossip and a good munch on what were by this point rather cold pumpkin sandwiches (though delicious nonetheless). No one was prouder of Cinderella than her fairy good-mother who was always watching over her and had written a special message for her in the stars.

# THE END*

*Well, actually it's just the beginning,
because there's still a lot of work to be done
before we live in a just and fair society.
But YOU can change the world.
YOU have the power.
YOU can do anything . . .

Just remember to always read the small print.